Twelve All in Dread

The Twelfth Witch and Other Stories

JULIANA REW

Cover Art by Keely Rew

Twelve All in Dread
The Twelfth Witch and Other Stories

By Juliana Rew

Published by Sophont Press
An imprint of Third Flatiron Publishing

Discover other titles by Juliana Rew:

The Adventures of Mountain Ma'am
Erenarch Academy: Under the Dragon Banner
Miranda of Daris
The Unwinding: Gin's Story
Extremophile: Violet Rain
Lucanus: Prodigal Son

We appreciate your reviews.

*****~~~~~*****

Cover: Keely Rew

www.julianarew.com

Contents

Part I: The Twelve All in Dread

Part II: Medieval and Modern Fantasies

*****~~~~~*****

PART I.
THE TWELVE ALL IN DREAD

The Twelfth Witch

Back home after another failed interview, Tessa riffled through the Help Wanted ads, looking for a paying internship. The last six applications had fallen through, and she was thoroughly discouraged and depressed.

So much for family connections, she thought. Her eleven sisters were all more than fully employed, and none of them had ever had to do apprenticeships. It was humiliating. It seemed that at every interview, the Hermetic Resources Specialist just wanted to pepper Tessa with questions about her famous siblings.

"Is it true that Norella and Hyperia can control the weather and stop rivers in their tracks?"

"Um, yes."

"Great Goddesses! Those would be useful skills we could really use. And I hear that Caledonia can play on a golden lyre and charm both young and old into the dancing fire?"

"Right. But technically it's the harp that does all the work."

"Well, witches with their own tools are in demand. Employers don't like to supply them. Most don't really like to train, either. They want someone ready to go on Day One. I've heard that your sister Morgana has her own grisly lindworm?"

"Well, yeah, although I'd call it more of a dragon."

"What a plus! I can hardly wait to hear what you have to offer, Tessa. We're really looking for help in the armaments area, you know, creating a blade that never needs sharpening, or clockwork soldiers that never run down."

"A perpetual motion machine has yet to be invented," Tessa pointed out. "I'm just looking for an internship so I can build my resume while I finish my studies." Companies were always trying to get poor grad students to work for cheap on open questions that even the greatest sorcerers had yet to figure out.

They would prattle on and on like that, right on down the list, until Tessa would finally cut them off, saying, "Yeah, yeah, yeah, their equals have not been seen on the face of the Earth." After that the interview would go downhill.

"We'll call you, Tesseracta," they would say. But they never did.

Tessa buttoned her icy hoodie up over her mail to cover her head against the freshening breeze. It was beginning to snow. Her mother had encouraged her to wear a warm cowl to the interview, but that was just too old-fashioned. You had to suffer a little for beauty. Well, actually, you didn't; it's easy enough to slap on some glamour. She had *some* integrity, for Goddesses' sake.

Flameit, she'd do anything to stop living in her parents' cellar, though she did enjoy the easy access to root-vegetable snacks. The smell of sulfur from her father's lab permeated her clothes, and it was impossible to get it out. But the job market was so bleak, she didn't know when she'd ever be able to get her own place.

On the way home, she had grabbed the latest job openings and had nearly given up on finding anything promising, when her gaze paused on the following:

SOLID INDOOR WORK. NO EXPERIENCE NECESSARY.

That didn't sound too bad. Not many details, though. She flicked a circle around it, sending an inquiry to the advertiser with her qualifications. She settled back to wait, stroking her familiar, Mnemonic Nick. Nick was a miniature dire corgi who could charm the pants off an angry berserker. Irresistible.

"Hey, Esmeralda," she said, giving her crystal mo-ball a shake and turning it over. The die within the ball bobbed briefly, then her best friend's face appeared.

"Hey, Belledame," Esmeralda replied. "How did the interview go?"

"Total debacle, as usual. I'm getting desperate. My only talent seems to be that I'm a vegetarian. That doesn't seem to bring the headhunters calling."

"Maybe you should become a cook. Your stuffed portobello mushrooms are to die for."

"Thanks. It's the leeks. But no, that's Nigella's bag."

"Have you talked to your advisor? I'd think he could find you something."

"Oh, he's all right, I guess, but I'd just like something more than these internship gigs …"

"More what?"

"Crazy."

"Crazy? Like exciting?"

"Yes, but also more cutting edge. And I don't mean keeping blades sharp. I mean really out there, where most people would think it's insane to go. Something new that would make me stand out from the crowd."

"Well, you've got the family genes for it. All your sisters have found a niche. Say, why don't you ask one of them?"

"Definitely not. It's got to be on my own terms."

"Sorry I'm not much help. I'm such a nerd, I just study all the time. Wait, maybe there's something in one of my books…"

Just then, the crystal flashed.

"I've got a call coming in, Ezzy. Call you back?"

Tessa broke the connection. "Yes?"

"Tesseracta Rowan?"

"Yes, that's me."

"I'm G. R. Penrus of Marmion Industries. Is this a good time?"

"Yes, certainly. I wanted to talk to you about your job ad."

"You are a fully qualified sorceress, are you not?"

"Of course! You've heard of the Twelve All in Dread, right?"

"Who?"

This was a first. This guy had never heard of the Rowan sisters.

"Um, could you tell me a little about the job? I'm a grad student, so I can't work full time, but I'm willing to take pretty much anything."

"Ah, excellent. You see, we mainly conduct covert operations, so anything we tell you must be held in the strictest confidence."

"No problem."

"In a nutshell, we assist parties desiring to break untenable contracts."

"Like what, for example?"

"Oh, escaping arranged marriages, runaway-bride rescue, that sort of thing. It's easy work if one is a witch."

"Is this legal?" Tessa asked, a little worried. She could just picture pitchfork-bearing families coming after her after she ruined their fifty-thousand-geltrangg wedding.

"Legality is rarely the issue for our clients."

"I see. You want some poor schlub of a rookie to do your dirty work for you."

"On the contrary. The work requires intelligence and the highest moral character."

"What about experience? Will you train me?"

"We expect you to rely on your best judgment. That's why we pay so well. Your credentials are excellent, so we are prepared to make an offer."

He scribbled on a small piece of paper and held it up to the crystal. The figure was a little distorted and blurry, but Tessa was finally able to make it out. Her mouth fell open. The pay was at least double anything she'd ever applied for.

Tessa knew that if something appeared too good to be true, it probably was. The whole thing sounded a little shady to her. But she was ready to try ever more lunatic things if it would get her that one-room forest cottage.

"Count me in, Mr. Penrus. I won't let you down."

"I'm positive about that, Tesseracta. Welcome aboard. Oh, and be sure to bring your armor."

"Penrus Escort and Security Service," said the voice at the other end of the mo-ball. "Please be advised this is not a secure connection."

Tessa hesitated. What was she getting herself into?

"I'm just calling to see when you want me to come in."

"One moment." The sound of lame muzak began to play.

"Tesseracta. Good of you to check in. We've got your first assignment all lined up. It's all in this heroic poem."

Tessa listened as Mr. Penrus described the case.

"You didn't tell me there were dragons involved."

"*Sleeping* dragons," Penrus stressed. "It is your job to make sure they don't awaken."

Right. Well, maybe she could go get some pointers from Morgana, in case the worst should happen. No. She was going to do this herself, and besides, she had her protective spells and armor. Should be a piece of cake. If she aced this assignment, there was even the chance of being promoted into the Twelve. She fancied herself as the greatest of them all—the Twelfth Witch Who Could All Things Understand.

On the pretext of having a date, Tessa borrowed her sister Euphorbia's earth-burrowing coach for the night. It had been slow going under the frozen soil, but shortly after midnight she arrived at the castle at last. The bitter chill of December poked inquiring fingers through the joints of her armor. An owl hooted in the trees nearby, sizing up a poor rabbit that limped in the frozen grass. A lone guard sat at the front gate, hunched over a tiny fire and obviously not expecting guests.

"I thought this was going to be indoor work," Tessa muttered, blowing on her hands to get some feeling back. "Best get inside and get it done."

The wedding guests were all within, Tessa knew, most fast asleep after the evening's prenuptial revels. She slipped by the guard with no trouble and entered the courtyard. Taking care not to step in any, she stopped briefly to enjoy the familiar perfume of horse manure and then spotted the arched portal leading to the chapel. That was where tomorrow's wedding would occur, and where the bride would undoubtedly be making her last confessions to the priest before retiring. As quietly as possible, Tessa clanked into the chapel. A pair of carved stone angels stood at the entry, their wings slightly unfurled, eager to enter heaven. Their beady eyes seemed to follow her as she crept in.

Tessa scanned the front pews for the bride. An old woman snored gently in the second row, her face pale.

The bride was nowhere in evidence. She must have left the chaperone to doze and gone off to bed. Tessa retraced her steps, exiting the great hall and heading for the sleeping quarters in the north tower.

Working her way down the second-floor corridor, Tessa finally found the bride's chamber. The girl sat bent over in a chair beside the bed, probably reciting one last prayer. Tessa made her move.

"Psst."

The girl started and looked up. She had been crying.

"What? Who are you?"

"I'm the one who's going to get you out of this fix."

"Oh, Lochinvar, I knew you'd come," the girl said. She held out her hands, which had been tied tightly.

I'm not Lochinvar! I'm a girl, for Goddesses' sake! Tessa thought, sticking her chest out. She had to admit, the armor didn't do much for her figure.

Tessa decided that this Lochinvar person was as good a disguise as any. She sawed away at the girl's bonds. "Like I said, I'm just here to take you away from your bloodthirsty relatives."

The girl blushed. This Lochinvar must be pretty hot.

"Did you talk with my father, Lochinvar?"

Brilliant, thought Tessa. "Let's go. Your true love is waiting."

"But it's a holy day," the girl protested. "St. Agnes's Eve."

"Don't worry about your reputation. Any who look upon us will see only your chaperone," Tessa said.

"Wait. You're not Lochinvar—you're a witch!" exclaimed the girl, opening her mouth to call for help but then thinking better of it.

"Tessa. Pleased to make your acquaintance," Tessa said, shaking her by the hand.

"I'm Maddy," the girl said. Suddenly Maddy's eyes widened slightly. Tessa twisted a bit to take a look, just enough to receive a glancing blow from the side. She fell to her knees in pain.

She must have blanked out temporarily, because when she awoke, she was lying on the ground looking up at a brown-robed priest with his foot on her throat.

"Aha, we've got you now, Lochinvar," he said. He held a heavy chalice in his hand. Tessa's tongue probed her rapidly swelling lip, tasting the metallic tang of sanguine fluid.

"Aagh," she said.

He lifted the cup to strike Tessa again. She struggled to escape, but the heavyset man had her pinned. Tessa glanced at her gauntlet, which was barbed with sharp spikes. She glanced at the priest's sandaled foot and made the obvious connection.

As the priest hopped about howling in pain, Tessa clambered to her feet. The angry man rushed at her again, and she held out her hands, grabbing his cowl and giving him a knee to the groin. She was glad she had taken that self-defense class. But it wasn't enough. It never was. His big hands closed around her neck, easily crushing her gorget and choking her. Hardly able to breathe, she made one last effort, thrusting her clasped hands upward to break his hold. As his hands flew away, she stood with her arms outstretched, and chanted. She wished to be rid of this troublesome priest.

The cleric's bulky brown robe disappeared, leaving him naked. He shrieked in embarrassment and did his best to cover his previously private parts. Then chunks of his face began to melt as if his skin had been removed, but there was no blood. His bones gradually disappeared, leaving only his internal muscles and brain dangling in the air. She was somehow sending parts of him *otherwhen*. What had she been chanting? Oh, yes, a *Begone* spell. The last of the man disappeared with a pop. He had probably gone to the future—or the past—and she had no idea when or if he'd be back.

Tessa grabbed the horrified Maddy, and they headed down the stairs of the tower, checking over their shoulders all the way. Tessa opened the door and propelled Maddy into the courtyard.

"Aarreeyah!" A dragon was chained to the front gate, barring their exit.

Tessa cursed under her breath. She should have prepared better. Even her full battle armor was ineffective against dragons. Theirs was the oldest magic.

She still had a splitting headache from when the priest had clocked her. What should she do?

"Umm, Maddy, why don't you go on back upstairs while I take care of this?"

Shaking, Maddy nodded. She turned and ran for the tower door.

"And watch out for the priest," Tessa called.

Her shout drew the dragon's attention, and it let loose a tongue of red-gold flame, just as a warm up. It would be pretty if it weren't so lethal.

"Nice draggy," Tessa called to draw the dragon away. She pulled out her sword and edged backward. Too late. Suddenly she was engulfed in flames. She dived behind a low stone wall, displacing sacks of sand and tossing them out into the courtyard.

Now she felt sheepish, getting roasted after traipsing unprepared into a dragon's keep. She sat down and tried to pull off her helmet, but her hair got caught in the visor, and she spent a painful few moments trying to untangle it. A wad of her black hair still stuck to the pin of the visor, punishment for her impatience. She rubbed her temples and folded her palms over her eyes. Images of fireworks had seared themselves onto her retinas, leaving her with flashbulb eyes.

The feeling of the armor was oppressively hot, so she clumsily undid the side buckles that reached from the waist up to the underarm. There must have been a dozen or more of them. Exhausted, she shed the breastplate and stripped down to her shirt of chain mail, burning her fingers. She ached all over from the night's exertions. She looked at her reflection in the pile of metal. What a mess. Her eyes were bloodshot, she was missing a tooth, and what was left of her hair was matted to her forehead. But mostly, she felt bad for the poor bride. She'd been deranged to take this assignment. She had totally bungled the extraction—and blown her chance at a promotion.

A mighty blast from a horn heralded disaster. *Well, that's it,* she thought. The whole castle would be swarming down on her shortly.

She cowered as the thunder of the dragon's footsteps approached the wall she was hiding behind. She was toast. Well, there was nothing for it except to do to the dragon what she'd done to the priest…

"Sit down and leave her alone, boy." *Morgana?*

Tessa peeked over the wall. Her sister was petting the dragon, feeding the kreatophagous creature treats of an unsavory nature. Her other sister Ettagorn stood nearby, her fingers idly playing over the pistons of her blarebugle.

"You can come out now. The mission's over."

"But I didn't succeed at all," Tessa protested. "The bride's still up there in her room, and everyone's waking up. I'm ashamed you had to come bail me out."

"We didn't bail you out, little sister. While you were creating a diversion, Lochinvar came in and stole her away," Morgana said. "Nice job tesseracting the priest, by the way. Good work."

Good work? Confused but grateful that her sisters had her back, Tessa exhaled and collapsed with a clatter. As she toggled in and out of consciousness, she heard her sister talking to someone on the other end of her mo-ball.

"She'll be fine, Penrus. She's just managed to get herself a little singed. It's no exaggeration when I say I think she has a great future." Although Tessa knew the mission hadn't come off exactly as planned, she appreciated her sister's attempt to bolster her confidence, and it didn't hurt that Morgana was taking this opportunity to engage in a little PR for the Twelve. So, Penrus *had* heard of the Rowan sisters after all!

"At least she's eager," he replied, not the least bit fooled.

"Hmm, this tomato-and-artichoke bruschetta isn't half bad," Tessa's father said, helping himself to another piece. "Must be the olive oil. So, what's this I hear about you getting a job?"

"You left out *'finally*,' Dad," Tessa replied.

"I didn't say that—"

"I suppose Morgana told you about the St. Agnes's Eve fiasco?"

"Well, it's a little hard to miss the new shaved hairdo. Doing the punk thing now, are we?"

"Can't we all just enjoy the lovely dinner Tessa slaved over all afternoon?" her mom piped in.

"I only meant—I just wanted to say that we're proud of you, Tesseracta. We know you can do whatever you put your mind to. You remember that's the Twelfth Witch's special talent, don't you?"

The grandfather clock bonged deeply in the hall. Tessa set down her fork and looked around. Her parents were positively beaming at her. Home still looked the same, but somehow it felt different—the crazy new something she'd been waiting for was here, too.

Tessa was beginning to all things understand.

"Questions?" asked the Great Frakulus, concluding his invited talk at the University. About forty students had trooped over to the Medallion Applied Sciences Building, endowed by the incredibly rich thaumaturgic megalopoly. They all hoped to get jobs with Medallion one day.

"Why do you want to replace phlogiston with natural gas, anyway?" a student asked.

"Glad you asked. Medallion feels that phlogiston's days are numbered. It's costly to extract and contributes to global warming. People just aren't willing to put their lives on the line for a pound of phlogiston any more. We have entered into an agreement to retrofit the entire dragon fleet with natural gas by next year. It will result in savings of over ten million geltranggs over the life of the contract."

The room burst into cacophonous booing and whistling. Tessa stood up and tried to restore order. She failed utterly, and the students streamed out of the hall muttering and jostling.

Tessa now regretted agreeing to introduce Frakulus while her advisor, Professor Randio, was away attending to pressing business.

"I do have thome projecth here that you could do to make a little ekthtra money," he'd said in his charming Castilian accent. As he'd stroked his familiar, Gus, Tessa's eyes had begun to itch and swell. She was deathly allergic to cats. "I realize it'th hard living on a grad thtudent thalary."

Tessa had agreed heartily. *I will probably never get out of my parents' cellar in this lifetime.*

"Goddeth bleth you," Randio had lisped, scooping up Gus and vanishing.

"That went well, didn't it?" Frakulus said. "That's what happens when you try to keep the public informed."

Tessa apologized and walked with him back to the quad. She waved good-bye as the tall figure twirled his cape and stepped backward into the shimmering freightflinger. He did not wave back.

She'd known the Great Frakulus's work had something to do with energy exploration, but she didn't usually pay much attention to such things. Earth-burrowing activities tended to be more her sister Euphorbia's bag. Besides, her father's experiments generated enough sulfur and gas to keep the household warm all winter. Except her room in the root cellar, alas. Luckily, she spent a lot of time puttering in her parents' kitchen.

Dinner was sautéed asparagus with hollandaise, one of Tessa's veggie specialties. Her secret weapon was a dash of Parmesan cheese. As she set the spoon on automatic to prevent the egg yolks from congealing, she mused over the afternoon's lecture. Just who was this "contract" with, anyway?

She pulled her crystal mo-ball from her pocket, gave it a shake, and turned it over. Wait until her sister Morgana heard about this. Tessa was pretty sure that nobody would be able to retrofit anything until the Twelve All in Dread approved. Well, they were only the Eleven so far, but someday Tessa hoped to reach her sisters' level of expertise.

The die within the ball bobbed briefly, then Morgana's face appeared. Tessa set the ball beside the stove.

"Hey, Morgana."

"What's up, kiddo?"

Tessa filled her in on Frakulus's seminar about Medallion's northern venture, ending with a breathless question. "So who do you think has this so-called contract?"

"Relax, dear. It's all under control. Except perhaps for the Pure Water Fund people. Penrus and I are negotiating with them now."

"But is it going to be safe for dragons?" Not that Tessa was overly fond of her sister's pets. Absentmindedly, her hand strayed to the bald spot she'd gotten on one side from yanking her red-hot armet off too quickly the other night. She'd been wearing the hood up on her cowlie all week to cover it.

"We'll never know unless we try," Morgana said.

Tessa felt a little better knowing that Marmion Industries and her sisters were on top of things. She wondered when, if ever, she'd be in the loop for breaking news.

"Which reminds me," Morgana said, "we'll need an escape clause on the contract if things don't work out." That was Marmion's specialty—covert operations and breaking untenable contracts. So maybe things weren't quite as copacetic as Morgana let on …

"What can I do to help? I've got the week off, with Professor Randio off *incommunicado* with something or other."

"We'd like you to go up there and check out the Medallion operation."

"Anything in particular?"

"As Penrus would say, 'We expect you to rely on your best judgment. That's why we pay so well.'"

Tessa started to grimace, but decided to maintain a poker face.

"There's my girl," Morgana said, breaking the connection. Tessa flipped the asparagus spears one last time with a spatula and pushed them onto a plate.

☯ ☯ ☯

Kekkonen Park was magnificent, no doubt about it. Just as the Great Frakulus had conjured in his presentation, three tall conical mountains like rabbit ears marked the boundaries of the park, surrounding a deep fell in the middle. High clouds stretched through azure skies, casting shadows over the gold-tinged heather. How anyone could allow oil and gas leases on the starkly beautiful moor was beyond Tessa. Nevertheless, she was there to get the lay of the land.

"Hello, young lady," a middle-aged man in a gray felted wool caftan greeted her. "Need a ride?" He pointed to his snowstrider and gestured for her to climb on behind.

"Where to?"

"The Medallion installation, if you please," Tessa said.

"You aren't one of those pesky Rowan sisters, are you?" the man asked.

"Why, yes, how did you know?" She decided not to take umbrage at the word "pesky." She often felt that way about them herself.

"You're not the first one to come poking her nose around here," he replied. "Just make sure you use protection."

I brought my armor, Tessa mused.

"Armor ain't gonna be enough," he said, as if reading her thoughts. "There's been a monster roaming about the fell."

"I'm sure I'll be fine." Tessa sniffed. "Please just get me there, before I look for other transportation."

"All right, hold your horses," he said, then took off with whiplash-inducing speed.

Within a few minutes, they pulled up to a chain-link fence topped with barbed wire and posted with signs warning that unauthorized personnel would be prosecuted.

"Thanks," Tessa said, peeling off what she thought was a generous twenty-geltrangg note. The man peered suspiciously at the money, as though it was foreign currency.

"I assure you, it's legal tender everywhere," Tessa said.

He shrugged, and the snowstrider galloped away as if pursued by demons.

Just beyond the Medallion enclosure sat a tall guard tower, apparently empty. Tessa crunched over the permafrost to the gate and pronounced the number Morgana had given her to her mo-ball. There was no answer. "Try again later," the die said. She decided to essay the intercom and leaned in to push the red button. She heard a soft snort as a cold, wet nose poked its way under her hand and pushed it away.

"Aww," she said. "A little reindeer." The waist-high artiodactyl was so adorable that it would give even her familiar, Mnemonic Nick, a run for his money. Her miniature dire corgi was a ten on the cuteness scale. She hoped her best friend Esmeralda was taking good care of him.

"Lady Tesseracta," the precious creature said, "Lady Greneth sends her greetings." That explained a lot. Greneth could tame all that in the greenwood crept.

"Grenny? She's here?" That was just her luck, flameit. As usual, one of her older sisters had gotten the jump on her.

"We must take care not to be seen. I will escort you through a rear entrance that is obscured by a stand of pines," the reindeer said. "There is something I must show you. Follow me closely."

"Okey doke," Tessa agreed.

"Not that close," it cautioned, pulling up lame.

"Sorry. Here, I'll go clear." She shuddered slightly, and her hoodie turned transparent, totally covering her torso and mail headdress. She crouched behind as the reindeer traced a torturous path designed to mimic random grazing.

"Is this where we'll find Gren?" Tessa asked.

"Shh. Lady Greneth is not here—she merely bade me bring you here."

"Sorry, my bad," Tessa said.

The reindeer shook its head. Apparently it didn't care for bad puns.

Wicked-looking thornbushes camouflaged a short flight of concrete stairs leading to a door into the compound. It was a little strange that there was no fence, but this certainly made things easier. Tessa clanked up the stairs as quietly as her sabatons would permit and pulled it open for the reindeer, but it was already gone.

"I thought you had something to show me… Why don't I just go on alone, then?"

She paused as her eyes gradually adjusted to the gloom. Just a big warehouse. No disguised gas wells or anything like that. Palettes lay stacked around the perimeter, probably supplies and construction materials.

Nobody home.

Wait. She heard sounds, like someone crying or moaning. She inched forward. The sounds grew a little louder. Spotting another door, she turned the knob and peeked in. A cry of anguish assaulted her ears, a bloodcurdling noise sufficient to raise a ghost. It was followed by a deafening rumble as the ground shifted under her feet. She scrambled backward. An earthquake? The grinding vibration abruptly subsided.

Her nerve returning, Tessa reopened the door and sought out the direction the sounds were coming from. The dungeon-like room stank of offal, like something the cat had rejected. A cage stood in its center, large enough to hold a prisoner or two, but at first Tessa couldn't see anyone. Suddenly a huge form crashed against the bars, its arms reaching out to claw at her. She stumbled back against a wood desk, nearly losing her balance. Claws? Definitely claws.

Tessa's protective spells seemed to be working, because the creature missed by a mile. Nonetheless, she began to see the folly in detouring from her appointed mission. But the desk and chair looked familiar somehow. She magicked open the top drawer. Snacks. Somebody liked Spanish peanuts. The growling grew louder, and she quickly moved on to the next drawer.

Ah, that was more like it. Rolled up maps, blueprints, and assay reports. She quickly stuffed as many as would fit into the front of her cowlie. She should probably get out of there in case there was another temblor.

"May I help you?" a voice boomed behind her. She spun around, spilling a couple of sheepskins. Thank the Goddesses. It was the Great Frakulus.

"Hello, sir, it's me, Tessa, from the university, remember?"

He scowled. "I should have known better than to let Joffrey do that lecture. And now that you've remarked everything, I'm going to have to kill you."

"Remarked everything? But I haven't seen *anything*," Tessa said, "and if I did, I wouldn't even know what it was." So this wasn't Joffrey Frakulus? If not, it must be his twin.

"Who are you, anyway?" she asked, when she knew what she should have been doing was sprinting.

The outsize man strode over to the cage and flung it open.

"You're not welcome in *my* legerdomain," he said. "Go get her, Dridfrodril!"

The hulking creature, which was like a cross between a tiger and a bear, screeched and leaped out of the cage, flattening Tessa before she had a chance to think.

Things must have gone black for a bit. She awoke to a crushing pressure on her chest. Her eyes itched horribly and felt nearly crusted shut. Eventually she divined that the predator standing on her chest was a feline, its paws denting her cuirass and compromising her breathing. She was deathly allergic to cats. Acid, dander-laden slobber dripped from the fiend's pointed yellow fangs. Tessa's nasal passages grew increasingly febrile, until with an involuntary spasm, her sinuses emptied themselves in a giant explosion.

Begone!

The creature's long furry coat disappeared. It yelped and began shivering. Chunks of raw flesh, eyeballs, and formerly tufted ears melted, along with paws with claws. Bones sheared away, leaving only pulsing organs dangling in the air. Like a drain satisfyingly cleared by a plunger, a final gurgling sound indicated that the ogre had been temporarily dispatched to some other dimension. Tessa couldn't be sure when the cat would return, so she began rocking back and forth in an attempt to right herself. Sometimes armor was more trouble than it was worth.

"You killed my familiar!" the man yelled.

"Well, actually…" Tessa began.

Just then, a new commotion ensued, and a second Frakulus burst into the room along with several guards. "Seize him," Frakulus Number Two ordered, pointing at his doppelganger with one hand and reaching out to assist Tessa with the other.

"It's little Miss Rowan, if I'm not mistaken." He tugged, and she lurched to a standing position.

The prisoner seemed to shrink before their eyes.

"Who are you, anyway?" Tessa asked again.

"It'th none of your busineth." That lisp was familiar.

"Professor Randio? What are *you* doing here?"

A blinding strobe raked the vault as the professor instantly vanished. Belatedly, Tessa shielded her eyes.

Life at the University seemed to go on as usual. Tessa had spent the last two weeks filling in for Professor Randio's Advanced Alchemy class, while the mystery of his disappearance at Medallion Industries' gas refinery retreated to the background. There was still the question of why he had set a beast prowling about the grounds, although it did help explain the lack of staffing around the place. Could it really be true that the shaggy brute was Randio's little tiger cat, Gus?

Her mo-ball signaled an incoming call. "Excuse me," she said to the class. "I've got to take this." She stepped outside and closed the door. It was Morgana.

"Hi, sis. Thought I'd fill you in on the Korvatunturi case. Good work, once again, scoring all those incriminating papers and tesseracting the Fiend of the Fell."

"But Randio escaped, Morgana, nobody knows where. I've failed in *another* mission, if that's what this was."

"Not at all. The documents you appropriated showed that Professor Randio was falsifying the results of the natural gas tests on dragons. Turns out they were a bust, and we're going to have to stick with phlogiston for the time being. Not to mention that all the pumping of frakwater into the wells is increasing seismic activity in the park. Hyperia was all set to stop rivers in their tracks so Euphorbia could tunnel through the earth to construct a pipeline. That's all on hold now, until we can get more data and thoroughly inspect everything for safety. Maybe there's even a scholarly paper in it for you."

"What about the fiend, then?"

"He's had to relocate and become the 'Monster of the Moor' or something. Doesn't have quite the cachet, does it?"

"Um, okay," Tessa said, willing to take "yes" for an answer.

"Oh, and before I let you go, we need a current picture of you to put in the Grand Hall alongside your sisters. Congratulations, you're officially one of The Twelve now. Talk to you soon."

Tessa'd finally found her special talent. *All things understanding.* She raised her mo-ball up to eye level and turned her head to the side. A nice, dignified profile, perhaps.

"Selfie rampant," she pronounced.

*****~~~~*****

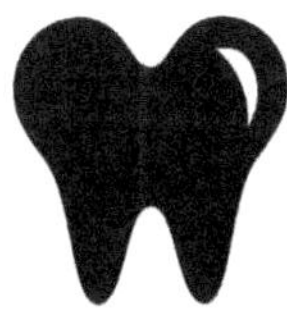

Ebony and Stainless Steel

Tesseracta Rowan's sister Morgana had warned her this might be a tough assignment. Nonetheless, she was simply dying to visit the tropical island of Guadeloupe. She'd finally scored a perk normally reserved for the Twelve Witches All in Dread. Besides, *somebody* had to do it.

Mnemonic Nick, Tessa's familiar, tilted his head. Adorable. It would hardly cost anything to buy her miniature dire corgi a ticket.

"All right, you can go," she said. The chunky little black dog jumped into her arms, and they headed to the freightflinger on the campus quad.

Seconds later, they stepped onto the sizzling tarmac of downtown Pointe-à-Pitre.

"Hope you won't be too hot, Nick," Tessa said. Corgis were double-coated, descendants of spitz breeds in the far north. She reached down to pat his "fairy saddle," the fluffy white fur covering his shoulders. Legend had it that fairies and elves had used corgis to pull their coaches and serve as the steed for fairy warriors. It was lucky that she stepped aside, as a three-wheeled Can-Am moto barreled by, nearly running them down. Bingo.

"That's her, Nick," Tessa said. "Let's go." They followed the moto to a shadowy storefront labeled "Le Dentiste" in faintly phosphoring letters.

Tessa's part-time job with Marmion Industries was to help break unbreakable contracts, and the girl riding on the back of the Cam-Am definitely was caught in one of those.

Inside, A turbaned woman in a kaleidoscopic dress sat behind the counter with a tiny black French poodle in her lap. Her little dog began yapping frenetically at Tessa, who followed in close behind the girl.

"*Tais toi*, Fifi," the receptionist said. "Welcome to Le Dentiste. Do you have an appointment?"

"Um, 'fraid not," Tessa said. She fingered the short sword on her belt.

"You can't do this," the girl was pleading. " When I signed the contract to get braces, you didn't tell me the braces were *vamp* braces. And your dog *bit* me."

"*Je suis désolé*," said the man in the white coat, who looked to be the dentist. "Fifi was just very hungry."

Desperate, the girl reached over and snipped a bit of hair off Fifi's poof. Tessa knew the hair of a black dog was a powerful charm.

Snarling, Fifi jumped down from the receptionist's lap and began growing to enormous size, metal teeth flashing.

Nick the corgi sprang to the girl's defense, never one to let a thing like size worry him. The battling dogs turned into whirling black bundle of aggression.

Tessa turned to the girl. "Hi, Fabrianne, right? I'm here to rescue you." Fabrianne looked grateful, but dubious. It looked like Nick was taking a beating, and Fifi was obviously a hellhound. A little worried, Tessa began to chant.

"Begone!" Fifi's fancy pouf disappeared first, followed by her skin and bones. Soon only her inner organs dangled in the air, before they too sheared away into another dimension. Fifi's bloody stainless steel teeth fell to the floor, apparently immune to Tessa's tesseracting skills.

As if they were a rat whose neck he wanted to break, Nick shook the teeth from side to side and beat them against the floor. Finally, he dropped them, raised his leg, and peed.

"Ew," Tessa said. "Er, I mean, good work, boy."

Back home in time for Halloween, Tessa called Morgana on her mo-ball.

"Hi, kiddo. How did it go?"

"Fine," Tessa replied. "I always take a dog to a witch fight."

*****~~~~~*****

Banish Mishanter

The asp viper tattoo on Tesseracta Rowan's forearm hissed. She'd forgotten to put it in vibrate mode. Hastily excusing herself and stepping outside the classroom, she fished her mo-ball out of the pocket of her cowled hoodie.

"Yel-lo."

"It's me." How come she didn't already know her sister Morgana called? She was supposed to be getting close to "All Things Understanding," wasn't she? The Twelfth Witch, indeed. Every sister of the Twelve possessed a special power. Morgana could control fire-breathing grisly worms, which at least seemed a tangible skill, unlike "understanding," which sounded rather vague. As the youngest, Tessa worried that her only skill seemed to be inadvertently tesseracting things into another dimension, and she certainly didn't understand that.

"'Sup, sis? Got a new job for me? I could sure use the extra geltranggs. They're increasing tuition here at the university, but not giving us teaching assistants a raise, as usual." She hoped Morgana would hire her to perform another clandestine mission for Marmion Industries.

"I'm afraid it's a family matter this time," Morgana replied. "One of our sisters is in trouble, or is about to be."

Damn. Tesseracta hadn't even had an inkling. She wracked her brain. Nigella? No, she never ate meat, which could be annoying, of course, but unlikely to get anyone up in arms, except their mother. Ettagorn? Her blare bugel could wake the dead, but she mostly only used it to herald significant events.

"Is it Hyperia? Has she caused another earthquake?"

"It's Caledonia."

Tesseracta drew a blank.

"The one in Scotland? I've never met her."

"Of course you have, dear. You were rather young when she moved. Now's your chance to visit her and get reacquainted."

"But this isn't a vacation, right? What's the problem?"

"You've heard the term, 'going native?'" Morgana paused. "Let's just say Caledonia is in a dangerous area for witches to be right now. "I've already loaded your armor and supplies on the freightflinger portal to Tulliniemi, and Nimue can take you the rest of the way across the North Sea."

🌀🌀🌀

A tall castle loomed over the coast of eastern Scotland, where an excited Tessa arrived with her sister to begin the new gig. The sun shone gold on the limestone, lending it the aura of a latter-day Camelot. They would be avoiding that, for sure. Tessa'd gotten detailed directions from a selkie about where to make landfall much farther north.

"You don't think Caledonia's become a selkie, do you?" Tesseracta asked her older sister. Of course not. Selkies were seal folk who could turn into people, not the other way around. She was getting her mythology mixed up. Nimue shrugged. She blinked at Tessa, her eyes rippling like azure pools.

"Not likely. She wouldn't want to get that precious harp of hers wet. It's just a short journey over land from here. Give me a call if you need help. I'm as close as the nearest body of water."

The Lady of the Lake checked her hairdo in a puddle before whisking herself home.

The freightflinger had delivered an imposing pile of luggage. Tessa supposed it must use tesseracting, and resolved to find out exactly how it worked so dependably when she returned home. She had no intention of lugging all that stuff on her journey, however. She would have to work her way west across the waistline of Scotland, to a tiny hamlet called Ayr, on the opposite coast. She wondered why Caledonia lived so remote from her sisters. Scotland was still considered "the North," of course, but only the very southernmost part.

Come to think of it, Caledonia's motives didn't seem so mysterious. The Rowan sisters could be a pesky, meddling lot. Except Nimue, who tended to be a loner, like her illustrious namesake in the days of King Arthur. Tesseracta felt slightly sheepish about coming uninvited to indulge in a family intervention. On the other hand, she wanted to show her older sisters that she could be a worthy member of the Twelve, an objective that had proved frustratingly difficult thus far.

She popped off her armet helmet to survey the scene. Morgana had insisted she take her armor, though no one wore the traditional uniform these days. A blast of icy air lifted her black hair into the sky, where it stood at attention as the wind beat on her face. She pulled up her cowl and tied it tightly under her chin.

"Who's this now, and wearing a suit of armor?" a voice boomed out. "Ain't you afraid of rusting?"

Tessa swore under her breath. They'd specifically asked that selkie for a place where no humans would be wandering about, accidentally spotting supernatural events. The witches obviously shouldn't have trusted her. Selkies tended to tell you whatever you wanted to hear.

"Good day to you," Tessa said with a slight bow. "I am visiting your fair shore from a foreign country."

"Whit country is that?" what turned out to be a very large ginger-haired man said. "You're all got up medieval."

"I came directly for the Renaissance Festival," Tessa improvised. "You have one here, don't you?" No matter that the Renaissance wasn't medieval. Humans typically didn't know the difference.

He laughed. "The only festival we have here is a flock of seagulls. Someone must be pullin' yer leg."

Seabirds?

"Ah, yes, I'm anxious to view some pelicans in their natural habitat, and I hear you have some fine ones here," she re-improvised.

Tessa couldn't believe the man actually fell for this. He began prattling on about the cormorants, boobies, gannets, and shoebills local to the area. Not to mention the puffins. Now puffins she could get behind, although her natural bird preference was jackdaws. They were like miniature dire crows. She liked dire things that were miniature. As if reading her mind, her little asp gave her arm an encouraging squeeze.

"The best sightings are on the Isle of Arran and around Alloway," the man said. The village is a wee bit inland, but the River Doon does bring in the seabirds."

Tesseracta looked for the sun for direction, but gray clouds hid the sky. She put the sea at her back and set off for the forested area in the distance. Keeping the mossy side of trees to her left should keep her on the right track. Miles inland, she reached the edge of a forest. A hand-painted sign posted on a trunk simply read, "MISHANTER."

"Misfortune," she translated from the Gaelic. She snorted. A cliché, warning superstitious humans to stay away from a haunted forest. All the better, as far as Tessa was concerned. Still, she began to feel uneasy. Pain jabbed at her forehead, as a sparkling aura flared in the corner of her eye. The emanation gradually grew until it blocked her vision. She could swear she heard a wailing baby and turned her head to try to find the direction it came from. Was this a premonition or a migraine? She often had both… A haunting tune teased its way forward from the back of her mind, one Caledonia had played often on her harp. Breathing deeply, she tried to calm her fear.

The vision gradually subsided, leaving her queasy and none the wiser about Caledonia's whereabouts. Probably the cry of one of the area's omnipresent seagulls had set off her headache. Tesseracta ignored the sign and entered the forest, making her way across a muddy, leaf-strewn woodland. The only misfortune she encountered was probably going to be ruining her good sabatons. That human hadn't been wrong about the steel foot coverings being susceptible to rust.

Eventually she emerged above a clearing. A line of farmers cut hay, taking advantage of the break in the rain. Tesseracta admired the charmingly old-fashioned scene, with no motorized machinery in evidence, only carts, rakes, and sickles. The humans looked harmless enough, so she unbuckled her breastplate and looked about for a place to stow her armor. She realized that for once tesseracting could prove useful. She wasn't exactly sure how to retrieve the armor—but she didn't need it at the moment.

Staying hidden and trailing at a respectful distance, the much enlightened Tessa followed the group toward the town of Alloway.

One jimmy in a blue hat said, "I'm stopping at the public house for an ale or a oueiskey. Anyone want to join me? What about you, poet?"

"Won't yer Kate be mad if you don't head straight home?" a handsome, curly-haired young man teased.

"Don't you worry none, Rabbie, I'm the boss in my own house," the man bragged. They all laughed. "There's a storm brewing. Kate'll have yer heid for sure," one retorted.

The setting sun broke through for a moment to reflect off the river cutting the town in half. Near the river sat an abandoned church, its roof open to the sky. Blackened rafters reached like fingers imploring heaven.

The men trooped into a thatch-roofed building on the sodden high street. A smoky fireplace dimly lit the inside of the public house. Tesseracta guessed the tavern was only slightly warmer than the bitter outdoors, but she decided that she couldn't enter the public house without attracting attention. This humidity was brutal, however, and the wind was picking up. She crept around to the rear of the building and found a few horses tethered. They'd be a source of warmth, at least, until the locals were fortified and ready to head home. She nestled up to a brown mare with the name "Meg" branded on its leather cheekpiece.

"You're a beauty, Meg. Your master must love you a lot," she said, patting the horse's nose. Meg tossed her head and whinnied.

"Shh," Tesseracta warned.

Hours later, the men were still drinking and talking loudly about everything but her sister Caledonia. The one called Tam bragged again, about how he feared no evil. His friends agreed, claiming if they ever encountered a witch, they'd put her to the stake. Tessa decided they hadn't seen anything but the bottom of a beer mug, and listening to their gossip wouldn't be getting her anywhere tonight, if ever. As the midnight hour approached, to avoid freezing to death, Tesseracta headed over to the partial shelter of the old ruined church. In the inky blackness of the new moon, she tripped over a treacherous grassy tussock, wrenching her ankle. An electric bolt of pain shot up her spine.

Flickering lights seemed to guide her as Tesseracta limped unsteadily along. Aurora Borealis, perhaps? No—the light shone out from the broken kirk windows. She wasn't the only one who'd planned to spend the night.

Strains of music wavered in and out, carried on gusts of frigid wind. A rather poor rendition of a hornpipe, called "Mad Jack's Caper," if she wasn't mistaken. The fiddler's tritones were catchy, but his musicianship was poor. "Just because you are using the devil's interval doesn't automatically make you a good musician," Tessa mumbled. "You'd certainly benefit by practicing with a metronome," she added.

Dismissing the thought, she peered into one of the windows to see the cause of the celebration. To her surprise, a coven of witches and warlocks danced around a fire at the far end. She was in luck. They'd surely welcome her. And they'd probably know where Caledonia was—Hold on, she spotted Caledonia, cavorting on the arm of a muscled, red-faced brute.

An array of coffins, one open to display the corpse of a hanged man with the noose still around his neck, lined the interior of the ruined Alloway kirk. Bloody body parts were scattered everywhere, and the stench was overwhelming. Three squawling infants lay trussed up like turkeys ready for the spit. Tessa trembled.

Tesseracta came from a coven older than Christianity, and she knew an unholy gathering when she saw one. That sort of activity—the kind associated with human sacrifice—had been abandoned long ago by her sisters in the far North. Of course, various flavors of dark witchcraft still existed, but the vast majority now followed the modern wiccan teachings of the Twelve. This must be a throwback, a return to now-repudiated corrupt practices.

Extremist religion could be tricky that way. The red-faced beast was undoubtedly the Devil of legend, and Tessa had no desire to meet him.

Tessa quickly administered a protective spell over the infants, then moved along the outer wall toward the fire to get closer to Caledonia.

The orgy intensified, as the fiddler sawed out a reel, "The Devil's Dream," at an insane tempo.

Rather than show herself, Tessa cast another summoning spell that would bring Caledonia outside of the kirk. As if sleepwalking, Caledonia broke off from her dance partner, lifted her harp, and stepped outside. Her monstrous companion glowered, but soon turned to another attractive, half-naked witch. "Come here, Nannie Dee," he commanded. She hitched up her cutty-sark undergarment and obeyed.

Outside, Tesseracta spoke to her sister.

"Caledonia, wake up. It's me, Tessa."

Caledonia blinked and looked around. "Tessa? What are you doing here?" Self-consciously, she fidgeted with her clothes, wrapping her bare shoulders in a paisley shawl.

"Apparently I'm here to talk some sense into you," Tesseracta replied. She still puzzled about why she hadn't received any hermetic signals from beyond regarding Caledonia. "What are you doing consorting with the Devil?"

"I— I remember playing my golden lyre..."

"I get that," Tessa said. "Your playing is so beautiful it can make people jump into the dancing fire. Just the place the Devil would like to see everyone."

"I don't remember how I got here, exactly," Caledonia confessed.

"Well, he obviously has the power to interfere with our skills. At least Morgana knew something was going on with you. I think maybe it's time to take a little break from Scotland, don't you agree? Get your harp, and I'll call Nimue to get us home. Which way to the river, Callie?"

Caledonia pointed in the direction of the River Doon. She summoned her harp and followed slowly. Very, very slowly. They had gone only a few steps, when Caledonia stopped and set her harp down.

"I don't think I can make it."

"Okay, spill," Tesseracta said. "I've got a bum ankle, and you're even slower than I am. You're stalling. What's the deal? I can understand why you're here, but what's with these lowlifes? You're one of the Twelve."

Caledonia sighed. "I needed some time to myself."

"Bull. If that were true, you could've let us all know, and we'd have respected your wishes. What, did you want to go find yourself?"

"No, it's not that. He said I could help with his big comeback. He needs me. And frankly I found life with the Twelve rather boring. I wanted some wildness, you know? What's the good of being a witch if you can't show off your powers? I can't just sit around studying all the time like you."

"Are you serious? Satan's big comeback? Uh… how did you know I study all the time?"

"Morgana told me."

"Oh... So, it sounds like you wanted to get away, but not so far that your sisters couldn't hear you. But you hadn't called lately, had you?"

"I loved the sense of control when I used the harp, and my new friends made me feel big, especially when I made a laughing stock of the dumb humans hereabouts. They told me I don't need to constantly be seeking my sisters' approval and asking their permission for every little thing. I don't think I want to go back."

Shattered, Tessa sat down. Her beautiful sister, lost? Callie's beautiful music, lost? She had one last chance.

"I completely ken that you want to be independent. Even if you love us, we can all be a bit much at times." She couldn't believe she was lumping herself in with her interfering sisters. "But could you play one more song for me before I go? I heard it in a tavern nearby. I think it they called it 'Auld Lang Syne.'"

Caledonia nodded, sat down, and began to pluck the tune, her voice sweet as warm honey. She sang a song of love, of friendship, of home, of yearning. Tears streamed from her face. The orgy in the kirk went silent, as the celebrants fell into a trance. Tesseracta ran into the kirk and stopped in front of the sept. These babies were not going to die tonight if she could help it.

"*Begone*!" she shouted. The infants vanished. Tessa wasn't sure where the tesseracted children would reappear, but it certainly wouldn't be in this hellish place. Tessa ran back out and pulled the reluctant Caledonia with her toward the river. They would make their final farewell there.

They were not quite halfway to the bridge over the River Doon, when they heard a terrible screech behind them.

"Uh, oh," Tesseracta said. "Looks like your boyfriend has discovered you've left."

"He's not my boyfriend," Caledonia objected. "— Exactly..."

As they turned to look back, a gray mare galloped toward them. Atop was that drunken farmer, Tam. What was *he* doing here?

"Run for your lives, lassies," he shouted. "I spied them in the kirk. It's the witches!"

Hot in pursuit followed the half-dressed witch, Nannie, along with another half dozen demons and witches.

"Let's move, Callie," Tesseracta urged.

"He'll kill me now," Caledonia observed soberly.

Tam lolled from side to side atop the careering equine and barely stayed aboard as Meg barreled toward them.

"Hold onto me," Tesseracta ordered, grabbing her sister by the shoulder. With unpracticed grace, she leapt onto the broad back of Meg behind Tam. Terrified, Meg reared and began to race even faster. With a loud crack, Tessa's armor popped out of thin air and wrapped itself around her.

Though a fine horse, Meg now bore three riders, and gradually began to flag. Nannie grew almost close enough to lay hands on Caledonia, who tried to fend her off with her harp. Nannie grabbed Meg's tail, and it appeared for a moment that the jig was up. Tesseracta debated whether to try to banish the witch to another dimension. But she was new at this sort of magic, and chances of a successful tesseract were unpredictable, not to mention that she and Caledonia would still be greatly outnumbered even if it worked. Then, to her shock, the horse's tail came off in Nannie's hand.

Luckily, they had reached the river bridge, where Tesseracta and Caledonia tumbled off, rolling to the water's edge.

Her load lightened, Meg clattered onto the bridge. The witch and her evil companions couldn't cross the water, and Tam would manage to escape with his life.

As the sisters scrambled to their feet, Tesseracta's armor abruptly tesseracted away.

"Brilliant," she said.

With a grin, Tesseracta pondered the rapidly retreating form of Tam O'Shanter and his gray mare, Meg. Maybe he'd ignored the "Mishanter" sign as well. Tam would have a lot to explain to his wife that night and for a long time after—especially what had become of Meg's tail.

Tessa turned to her sister. "I'm sorry to trick you into breaking with these so-called friends. Guess I'm merely here to do Morgana's dirty work, eh? Forgive me?"

Caledonia frowned, her irises growing dark. "I liked it here in the past, so it'll be hard. Someday, I'm sure."

"The past? I thought things seemed different, but I only thought I was fetching you from Scotland."

Callie sighed. "Scotland Seventeen Ninety."

Gazing into the turbulent river, Tesseracta was glad she and her sisters were immune to a superstitious fear of water. In fact, water was Nimue's specialty. She only hoped Nimue could locate them.

"Nimmie! Come get us," she called.

It might be after the fact yet again, but Tesseracta *was* beginning to All Things Understand. The Devil was real, and Caledonia had fallen into league with him. It was quite possible she'd need her sisters' help to fight back. Call it meddling if you wish.

As the Lady of the Lake's arm reached out for her sisters, Tesseracta resolved to return to Scotland someday. She hadn't gotten to see any puffins.

*****~~~~~*****

Outlook Good

Tesseracta Rowan's hands grew slippery as she kneaded suet into balls to feed the murder of crows adopted by the family over the years in the back garden. In case anything edible (or not) were to be dropped, Mnemonic Nick the dire Corgi splooted alertly, soaking up the sun at Tessa's feet. A flurry of shadows flitted across the kitchen floor. The birds must be eager.

Tessa scattered birdseed onto the kitchen counter to roll the suet in, her elbow inadvertently nudging her mo-ball.

The heavy black glass orb seemed to jump into the air, spiral slo-mo over and over, and finally crash to the floor. The mo-ball was a *gomboc*, and it was never supposed to fall, no matter how hard you hit it. It had some sort of gyroscopic thingamajiggery inside.

The ball rolled to a stop on the soft linoleum and perched precariously with its fortune window facing up. The icosahedral die inside bobbed to the top.

"I hope it's not broken," Tessa muttered. She tried to check whether any of the viscous black liquid that filled the mo-ball might be leaking.

SIGNS POINT TO YES.

Tessa read, tilting her head sideways. *Yes, it's broken? Or yes, it's fine?* "I guess I must have put you too close to the edge of the counter."

Tessa reached to pick it up. But the nearly round globe seemed to evade her grasp, staying just beyond her reach. If anything, it acted tipsy.

Tessa depended on her mo-ball to keep in touch with her friends, and more importantly, her sisters. The Twelve kept abreast of the latest technology. To the uninitiated, mo-balls were indistinguishable from playthings. But they were actually quite expensive, since they were crammed with condensed magic. Her father called it a "mass storage device," whatever that was. The whole family used gombacs to back up all their senstive thamaturgical data. Tessa even kept all her sister Nigella's recipes there. Along with her own, of course. Nigella was strictly vegetarian.

Maybe she should take it to her father for a look-see. No, that would show a lack of proper care. Besides, Tessa was the one who was supposed to understand everything. Unfortunately, that didn't always seem to be the case. She was still a work in progress.

"All right, I get that you're doing this on purpose, so come here and explain it to me." Tessa applied an attraction spell, and the mo-ball began to roll slowly toward her. As soon as she let her guard down, though, off it went, zipping out the back door faster than the eye could see. A thin trace of ebony liquid remained on the tile. Uh, oh, it was hurt, after all.

She sighed. She had class today, and this was going to make her late for the class she led as a teaching assistant while finishing up her graduate thesis. She dabbed a bit at the slime trail to clean up and bent over the sink to rinse the cloth. She felt a sting. Acid drops splashed upward into her face. Her eyes began to burn, and blinding her. With a scream, she abruptly vanished.

Morgana inspected her sister's basement apartment, which smelled pleasantly of sulfur from their father's phlogiston experiments. Tessa's tiny bedroom was empty, save for the unmade feather bed and pile of dirty clothes. Upstairs, the kitchen floor was strewn with birdseed and suet balls.

"Tessa never showed up at the University today," their mother said. "We're quite worried."

Morgana pulled out her own mo-ball and tried to reach Tessa. No reply. That was odd. Tessa was usually tied to the thing. Next, she tested for Tessa's presence in the world. No Tessa in this dimension. Perhaps she had tesseracted. That was one of Tessa's skills, after all. But she normally didn't tesseract herself, just other people and things. Morgana slipped the gomboc back into her capacious sleeve.

"I wouldn't worry too much, Mother," she said. "Tessa's probably just forgotten she had class. I'll let you know when we find her. Meanwhile, I'll just tidy up this mess a bit."

A sharp "caw" from outside caused them to look up.

"Do you think the crows saw anything?" their mother asked. "They were waiting patiently for their food…"

Tessa stood alone in a white room. It wasn't a room, exactly. It was a big *nothing*—except for air. It was like being the last yogurt in an empty refrigerator. She guessed she was between dimensions. Her eyes seemed to be working fine again, though they felt a bit raw. The question was, what was she seeing—or not-seeing? She felt her chest tighten and her tongue go numb. She listened for any sounds, but it was quiet, although perhaps she could feel her heart speed up. She told herself not to panic. If this was one of her involuntary tesseracts, she had found that they were usually protective, albeit unpredictable. Tesseracts were nonlinear, so she had no way of determining precisely when she would snap out of it back to the real world.

She looked down. She wore her usual university "uniform," a caped hoodie and jeans, but her clothes seemed to be faintly glowing. No mo-ball in sight.

But wait. There was a fuzzy dark object about the size of her device materializing nearby. Thank the goddesses. She'd take the thing in for a full tuneup as soon as she got back. Time to restablish dominion over her world. But when she tried to grab it, her hand passed right through it, like an icy fog.

She waited. And waited. It was her mo-ball, all right. But it wasn't fully materializing, like when your computer showed a progress bar that never seemed to move.

"Come here, dammit," she said. It not only did not come to her, it seemed to fade a little bit. Negative progress? This was intolerable, after all her work to become an expert communicator.

"Come on," she said again. The ball faded a little more. Worse, her clothes began to fade as well, and she could see her toes through her shoes, as if they'd been X-rayed. She began to worry that she was stranded at the intersection of Nowhere and Noplace. She'd once heard that X-rays could damage gombocs and delete magical data. That's why no one ever put them in their luggage when flying on a plane. Without her mo-ball, she considered how she could call one of her sisters or her best friend Esmeralda.

She called out to her sister Morgana, the strongest of the Twelve.

"Hello? Sis? Can you hear me? I've tesseracted, and it's taking unusually long to undo itself..."

For a while, there was only the same silence, then gradually followed by a low-pitched, static sound. Another fuzzy, dark object began to appear. Ah, some progress at last. But it wasn't her sister, it was much smaller. Not a gomboc, either. It looked like...

A crow.

Well, there's some company at least, Tessa thought. Perhaps the gomboc's wires had become crossed. Although, it didn't really have any wires. It was time to send out a distress signal.

"Concentrate," she told herself. She'd reach out mentally to Greneth next, since Grenny could tame all that in the greenwood crept. Once Grenny had helped Tessa sneak into a barbed-wire enclosed Russian military compound while crouched behind a reindeer. Of course, this wasn't the greenwood; it was more like the whitewood.

When she didn't hear from Grenny, she tried Euphorbia, who could tunnel through the earth. Was she even on the Earth? Euphorbia had helped Tessa burrow under a castle wall to help her free a young woman being forced into an unwanted marriage. Perhaps she could reach Nimue, who could dive in the sea like a fish, or Taika, who could dance on the rolling sea, or Hyperia, who could stop the torrents' rush.

Unfortunately, there didn't seem to be a drop of water in sight. That was too bad, because Nimue could whisk her anywhere there was even a small puddle. She'd helped Tessa get to Scotland to rescue her sister Caledonia from the Dark Lord...

Tessa was really missing her sisters, which was unusual for her. She'd tried so hard to crawl from under their fame by establishing her own power and reputation.

She peered at the gomboc, which showed little sign of solidifying further. Her father had once told her to always be aware that the thing was simply that—a thing— and to not become too attached to it, useful as it was for communication and data storage.

"You can't apply human characteristics to a purely mechanical object," he'd warned. That's called 'personification.'"

Tessa had objected, asking what about the animal familiars that all the witches had. They were more than just pets.

"Yes, they are living creatures, like us," her dad had pointed out. "But *you* should be able to physically tesseract whatever you want, whether animal, vegetable, or mineral," he said with a smile.

Maybe her dad was wrong about her being able to tesseract gombocs. Of course, she wasn't sure if her predicament was the result of a tesseract to another dimension. If the mo-ball wasn't going to help her out of this, she'd try locating another sister, Norella, who could hush storms. Maybe she was caught in a whirling blizzard. The white void responded with further silence. What about Elvira, then? She never slept. She was bound to hear her, right? Tessa was beginning to get hungry, recalling forlornly Nigella's tempting vegetarian masterpieces.

There were so many magical skills among her sisters. Why were they so different from each other? And why was she unable to reach out to her family?

She sat down and put her head in her hands. A strange, sucking, sound made her look up. It sounded like someone slurping on a milkshake through a straw. Rather alarming, actually. She tried to zero in on the sound, and noticed that it was indeed some sort of gooey liquid. But it wasn't the same as the black liquid inside her mo-ball.

With a high-pitched shriek, she realized it was a bloody piece of brown cloth, wet with blood. Blood mixed with flesh. Tessa recognized part of the body of the priest that she had tesseracted on her mission to save the unwilling bride. With horror, she watched as the priest's hair, bones, and skull, and eyeballs appeared. Sobbing, she shrank away from the pile of body parts. But the pile began to glow and gradually diminished. Though she was grateful for the respite, she at first didn't understand what had happened.

Then the sucking sound came back. Dreading the reappearance of the priest's banished body, she was surprised to see that, instead, a tail and fur and claws plopped onto the floor at her feet. This was undoubtedly from her battle with the fiend of the fell, which she had banished previously. Holding her breath, she waited, and, sure enough, the catlike body parts began to glow and diminish, followed by the appearance and disappearance of a curly black poodle who had turned out to be a hellhound. So, this was where her Begone spells sent their unfortunate victims.

The consolation was that people and things she'd banished almost always reappeared back in the real world. Nobody died, really. No harm done, right? A new thought crystallized.

Tessa was beginning to understand that her real skill was subtracting evil, adding happiness, and returning an improved version of consciousness, even if sat first he wasn't doing it intentionally. The universe she had always assumed to be either hostile or neutral was actually fluid and modifiable, for the better. This is what her magic really was. A civilizing skill.

But this new understanding wasn't helping her get out of this "white room." Communication was an equally important skill, and it need not be magical.

"Diminishing returns," Tessa said, discouraged. Nothing from Nigella, Nimue, Elvira, Caledonia, or Taika. Not even her blast to Ettagorn had any effect, although the crow seemed to flap its wings and caw several times.

"What is it, boy? Are you trying to tell me something?"

The crow, now fully materialized, fluffed its glossy black feathers and tilted its head from side to side.

"Are you hungry too, boy?" Tessa asked.

The bird hopped over to the mo-ball and pecked at it. Tessa laughed, and to her joy, the gomboc became solid.

"Yes!" Tessa cried. "Am I about to succeed at last?"

OUTLOOK GOOD.

—the ball read. A gust of wind blew her hood back, and Tessa found herself back in the kitchen. Her thirsty eyes drank in a blessed rainbow of colors.

Mnemonic Nick barked. Surprised and practically deafened, Morgana looked up, nearly dropping a dustpan full of birdseed. She set it down.

"Ah, you're back. What's going on?"

"Oh, nothing much," Tessa replied. "Just a little glitch in my mo-ball."

"We were worried about you," Morgana said, eyeing the shiny black corvid that had appeared with Tessa and was greedily pecking at the feast in the dustpan. "For a minute, I could swear I could hear you calling, but there was nothing on my mo-ball."

The sound of footsteps approaching the kitchen interrupted their conversation. Tessa opened the swinging door. Ten of her sisters squeezed in, talking animatedly.

"Did you call me?" they were all asking.

"Why—yes, yes, I did," Tessa said, extemporizing. Time to celebrate. "I've got a ton of day-old chocolate oatcakes, and I was hoping you could join me to polish them off, before they get stale."

There was another knock. Tessa's mom and dad stood there, seemingly asking permission to enter their own kitchen. "You call, dear? My, what a crowd," her mother said. "Why don't we all go outside? The rowan trees are going crazy this year, and the crows will beat us to all the berries if we don't pick some for ourselves."

"Excellent idea," Tessa said.

Smiling as her family clambered out to devour her oatcakes, Tessa felt glad to be back. She loved them all so much. And she'd understood something new today. Sometimes it took all Twelve to bring back the magic.

But it seemed like her gomboc's rebellion had ended when it ran away and bonded with a crow. Contrary to popular opinion, there appeared to be more than one kind of intelligence.

"While you're here, Dad, would you mind taking a look at my gomboc? It's been acting up a bit lately. And did you know crows can tesseract?"

*****~~~~~*****

Snapdragon and Foxglove

Tesseracta Rowan, rising star of the mystical world. At least, until lately.

After making her breakthrough into clairvoyance, the sky had been the limit. She'd taken her rightful place among her sisters, each of whom had fantastic powers of her own. The *Twelfth* Witch, admittedly, but well worth waiting for. Tessa had been the best and last, everyone said. The University eagerly patented her conjures, and she eagerly discovered them, one by one, although mostly by accident.

Tesseracting, named after her primary talent of banishing troublesome things to other worlds and times, had become unreliable, leaving Tessa perplexed. Now she didn't know if she would *ever* All Things Understand.

Too proud to admit it to her sisters and ask for advice, she noticed them whispering when they thought she wasn't looking. Caledonia's hisses were especially audible. Callie had lately fallen into evil company and was probably resentful of being kept on a tight leash by The

Twelve. Luckily, Tessa's eldest sister Morgana still talked with her daily, acting as if nothing were amiss.

Tessa thanked the goddess that whatever had gone wrong didn't appear contagious. There were few enough witches and wizards without a new plague spreading through the small Coven of the North. Maybe it was something paraphilosophical. She'd heard the Sight could be a tricky thing.

It was a rare day of Sun, so between early spring sleet storms Tessa borrowed a wooden bowl from her mother's kitchen and stepped outside to collect dandelion greens for a salad. She drank in the lovely smell of petrichor—the oils released from the earth after the recent rain shower. A profusion of bright yellow blooms cheered her as she judged which of the toothed leaves would be tenderest.

She reached for her gardening knife to dig out a group of fresh blossoms, but the knife eluded her grasp. She squatted in front of her target and tried again. Another miss.

"What is this?" she muttered. "Maybe there really *is* something wrong with my Vision. I'll ask Father to give me an eye test."

The sky darkened, and the wind felt chillier. The dandelion blossoms furled themselves into tight green balls as if they no longer wanted to be seen. Tessa knew exactly how they felt. Even the vegetables would have nothing to do with her. Neither would the knife, evidently. It rose from the ground and poised itself mid-air with the sharp point at chest level. Her armor, unbidden, wrapped itself around her body as the knife flew at her. The stabbing blade bounced off her cuirass and fell to the ground, where it disappeared in a shower of sparks.

She hadn't seen it coming. Tessa sighed, and a tear escaped down her cheek. Things hadn't been working right lately. This never would have happened if her miniature dire Corgi familiar Mnemonic Nick had been here to bark the alarm. She flipped up her cowl and retreated indoors.

Leaving a few wilted greens on the counter, she scrubbed the dirt off her hands and descended to the cellar. Her father was hard at work making some sort of sulfurous compound in his laboratory. She wrinkled her nose and changed her mind about disturbing him.

She tesseracted her armor off, then back on. At least that still worked, if intermittently.

She called up to her mother, "I won't be home for dinner tonight. There's something I need to do."

"All right, dear. Don't be too late."

Tessa clanked over to Morgana's place, giving her sister's chained-up grisly lindworm a wide berth. Dragonfire could melt even the strongest armor, as she'd once found out to her dismay.

Before the second knock, Morgana answered the door, raising a dark eyebrow at Tessa's armor, which was missing one sabaton and a shoulder cop. They had blinked off on the way over.

"Come in. I was just talking to Penrus. What's happened?"

"Oh, nothing, really. I could use something to do. You know…"

"Yes, I do know. You're hurting, and the grief is messing with your head. I was crushed when I lost my first familiar. They're such a part of the family."

That wasn't precisely what Tessa'd meant. She simply needed an assignment, a mission. Besides, she didn't think a dragon was quite the same thing as a familiar. A familiar had your back when times were tough, while dragons were overkill. Tessa remembered the time she'd been assigned to rescue a hapless Carolingian beauty from her unbreakable contract with the vampire Ledontiste. Tessa'd nearly lost it when Ledontiste's little black dog, Fifi, snarled and grew to enormous size. Mnemonic Nick sprang into action, nipping at the heels of Ledontiste's toy hellhound.

"I'll drink you for breakfast, you fat piece of blood sausage," Fifi roared, whirling around to protect her hind quarters from being turned into dire-Corgi hamburger. Though he was indeed short and slightly pudgy, Nick had big teeth for his size, and had learned to duck under many a demon's otherwise fatal kick. The two dogs fought furiously, until distinguishing them became almost impossible. Black fur flew in all directions.

"That'll do, Nick," Tessa said. The black cloud continued to roil.

"Nick!" Tessa yelled. "Stop! Now!" Nick broke off, but Fifi lunged again. Tessa screamed.

"*Begone!*" Fifi's fancy pouf disappeared first, then her skin and bones. Inner organs dangled in the air, before they too sheared away to who-knows-where. Its vampire teeth fell to the floor, seemingly immune to tesseracting.

Nick pounced, shaking the teeth like a rat. Finally, he dropped them, raised his leg, and peed.

"Ew," Tessa said. "Er, I mean, good work, boy."

After he'd defeated Fifi, Nick grinned adorably, as all Corgis do, and waited for a treat.

While not as deadly as a dreadful dragon, Nick had bought her the time she needed to save the damsel, and they had made it back home in plenty of time for All Hallows' Eve. It was a good memory. And it hurt.

Tessa's stomach clenched, and she felt a sour taste in her mouth. It seemed Fate had twisted a knife in her gut after all. All this had brought back the reminder that Nick had unexpectedly died of a sudden ailment.

That was six months ago. She should be over it by now, shouldn't she?

"I've got just the thing to take your mind off things," Morgana said.

"It's not a pet dragon, is it?" Tessa said.

"Oh, no, you'd never be able to handle that," Morgana said with a smile.

"And not a cat. I'm not really a cat person." She was actually deathly allergic.

"Of course not," Morgana said. "Just a little unfinished business from a past assignment. Go home. I'll give you the details tomorrow."

Tessa didn't get a chance to mention that her gardening knife had tried to kill her.

The asp tattoo on Tessa's arm buzzed, signaling a summons. She pulled her scrying ball from her bell sleeve, shook it, and turned it over. The obsidian icosahedron inside bobbed briefly and displayed the callerID: MOTHER OF TWELVE

"Hello, Mom?" Her mother's worried face emerged from the inky liquid.

"Tessa, where are you? Morgana's been in an accident. You've got to come home."

"Sure, I'll be right there," Tessa said.

But she wasn't right there. She felt afraid, inexplicably rooted to the spot. Eventually, she cajoled her body into walking home from the University. She should have gone right home like Morgana said, but she'd gone to her lab for a little peace and quiet while she contemplated her waning powers and shaky security.

"Morgana's been injured by her own lindworm," Tessa's mother said, wringing her hands. "We called Greneth, and even she had trouble getting the dragon to stop running amok, burning everything in sight. Finally, she had to put her down. It's a tragedy. She had just had a new brood." That was shocking—and strange. Normally Greneth could Tame All That in the Greenwood Crept.

"Is Morgana all right?" Caledonia poked her head into the room.

"Yes, no thanks to you," Tessa said.

"What do you mean by that?" Callie said.

"You've been mad since we curtailed your adventure with the Devil. Are you trying to take revenge on us?"

"Hell, no," Caledonia said, flatly denying the accusation. "I would never hurt any of you. Mother, tell her."

"Yes, that's right, Tessa. Callie has been working hard on her rehabilitation. It's not fair to blame her. This is much more than simple sibling rivalry."

"I'm sorry, I shouldn't have accused you," Tessa apologized. Even so, two of her sisters seemed to be having the same trouble that Tessa was. What wasn't she seeing?

Could magic be disappearing from the frosty North? As far as Tessa knew, Norella could still hush storms, Hyperia could still stop rivers in their tracks, and Elvira could still get by on zero sleep. Most of the family continued to do everything they'd always been able to do. Except Tessa. And now Morgana. And maybe Grenny.

Greneth said, "Morgana's resting now. Father gave her a sleeping potion. She was crying and mumbling incoherently about a familiar plot." Tessa had never seen Morgana cry about anything, and she hoped she never would. She shivered.

A plot. What sort of plot? As in a play, or something more sinister, as in "the plot thickens?" And against whom? The Rowan sisters? She ticked through The Twelve, and only the three with familiars or animal connections were affected.

A plot against familiars.

👁️👁️👁️

Tessa trudged to Morgana's lands at the edge of the pine forest, carrying a tightly sealed tub of carrion. Sealed or not, it smelled horribly rotten. The trees nearest the house were nothing but tall shards of charcoal. Alongside Morgana's house lay the immense form of her beloved dragon, its normally glassy eyes dull and staring.

Red antirrhinum, the dragons' flower, poked through the icy ground all around it, though unplanted by anyone. As if waiting for the proper witness, the dragon's corpse decomposed rapidly, disappearing among the florets. The snapdragons then shriveled, leaving no trace of Morgana's once-mighty monster. Tessa swallowed. When Morgana woke, someone would pay. Meanwhile, Tessa would be babysitting the adolescent hooligans.

"I guess I should get to it," Tessa said. Holding her breath against the stench, she slipped into the dragon coop and opened the lid. Three iridescent-scaled dragonets swooped down from their roosts, drawn by the alluring scent.

"Nice draggies," she said, hastily setting the jar down, backing away, and closing the gate. She exhaled and removed her helmet, relieved that the little buggers hadn't decided she was today's lunch. Yet, she missed feeding little Nick his breakfast of mastodon pie. She'd never been able to turn him into a vegetarian like her.

As she watched her sister's pets finish their meal, she sensed a cold wind working its fingers underneath her armor. Whatever it was, was back. She reached for her helmet, then everything went white.

When she woke, she discovered she couldn't move. Again. This time, she lay face down, with a heavy weight pressing from above. Petrichor wasn't so pleasant this close up. She stuck out her tongue and felt her helmet. Though tardy, at least it had made the effort. The noseplate provided a tiny space with air, but she knew she would soon suffocate.

With a last claustrophobic gasp, Tessa tried the spell that had saved her in the past.

"*Begone!* Please…"

As she slipped into unconsciousness, Tessa thought she heard a slight scratching sound. Probably someone coming to finish the job...

🐛🐛🐛

"Hello, little sister. You awake? Welcome back." Tessa was in her own bed. Morgana leaned over her, a bowl of soup in hand.

"Is that for me?" Tessa asked. It smelled really delicious. Leeks and rutabaga, undoubtedly.

"Nope, it's got chicken," Morgana said. "Don't you want to know why you're still alive?" Morgana said.

At Tessa's disappointed look, she laughed and said, "Oh, I see you vegetarians have your weaknesses, too." She handed over the bowl. "I suppose you can eat while I talk. May I introduce you to Bayard? He's responsible for digging you out of that little pickle you found yourself in."

Bayard, a twenty-something with a reddish beard, replied cautiously, "Not completely. You see, I came upon this arctic fox busily digging away near Morgana's house. Then, all of a sudden a volcano erupted, spraying frozen dirt ten feet into the air. That's when we saw you."

"We?"

A pure white fox jumped onto Tessa's bed.

"This is the fox," Bayard explained. "Apparently he thinks you're his now."

"So the tesseract *did* work," Tessa said. "But why? It hasn't worked properly in weeks." Morgana shot her a warning glance.

"Well, thank you very much, Bayard," Morgana said, taking him by the arm and propelling him toward the door. "We're very grateful to you. Now, Tessa needs her rest."

"Yes, thank you," Tessa said. She didn't see any need to rush the handsome Bayard out the door…

When he had gone, Tessa said, "I have this theory that someone is trying to kill us and our familiars."

"Your theory is correct," Morgana said. "When I consulted with Penrus about a new assignment for you at Marmion, he warned me that the subject of one of our ex-clients expressed outrage with our breaking of his unbreakable contract. He threatened severe punishment of the witches he held responsible. I won't repeat his language in front of polite company, but suffice it to say Mother read his heart and identified him as the perpetrator. His way of weakening you and me was through our familiars. He might have once had a case, but now he's in *rikkoutumaton* chains, thinking over his misdeeds."

"So this person may have killed Nick and your dragon?"

"I'm afraid so—"

Tessa didn't even want to think about it. Her armor abruptly wrapped itself around her.

"Seriously? Now?" she said. The armor went away.

Misunderstanding, Morgana added, "Yes, but look who's come to replace Nick. Your powers are clearly on the mend, now that you have a new familiar, I'd say."

The fox inched closer to Tessa and began to stalk her bowl of soup.

"Oh, no you don't, Valkoinen," Tessa warned.

"*White*. See, you've already named him."

Tessa's fingers idly brushed against Valko's snowy ruff. He was white now, but he'd be turning brown with the coming of summer. She loved him already … A hole inside her was beginning to fill again. She looked at her sister. Morgana was so brave, braver than she had been. "I'm sorry about your dragon," she said.

"I know, kiddo. How about you two walk me home?"

👀👀👀

A carpet of white flowers bloomed near Morgana's gate, nearly hiding the burn marks. "Look, the snapdragons are coming up white," she said.

"Those are foxglove," Tessa said. "They're closely related."

"How did you know that?"

"I don't know, it just came to me."

Morgana's three dragonets squealed with joy to see her. Valkoinen growled, defending his mistress from the rear.

Though Consciousness was already more bearable with a new familiar to share it with, Tessa recognized that her mischievous new friend was mortal. She'd never really get over Mnemonic Nick, but, like Morgana, she would somehow find the strength she needed to view a way forward.

Love was simply another piece of the puzzle of All Things Understanding.

*****~~~~~*****

Your Mother Should Know

Tesseracta Rowan and her mother, Skye. showed the other eleven sisters out after the family barbecue. Morgana had offered to help clean up, but Skye demurred, telling her eldest daughter to head back to her forest cottage. "You deserve a rest, dear. I'm sure your little dragonets are hungry. Tessa and I can handle it."

With Morgana gone, Skye collapsed into a kitchen chair and snorted. "I'm the one who could use a rest," she said, "and Morgana can be a lot… even when she's trying to be helpful. Her hatchlings would probably burn down half the kitchen."

Tessa chuckled and pulled out another chair to join her mom at the table. After she settled in, a big loose leaf binder flew off the shelf and fell open in front of them.

"Your recipe collection, Mom?" Tessa asked. "You know, you can keep all your recipes on a mo-ball and save a lot of shelf space."

"No, it's not a cookbook," Skye replied. "But speaking of space, I'd say you've hit the nail on the head."

"A book about space?" Tessa asked, puzzled. She gazed at the open page. Embossed in gold over an image of a red oak leaf was her name. "Oh, a family tree, then."

"It's time you knew about your true heritage," Skye said. "I told your father and the rest of the family that I should be the one to tell you. There's a reason you've had so much trouble fitting in."

Tessa felt glad to be sitting down. She guessed what she was about to hear. She was dark-haired, while her mom had wavy blonde locks. "You mean I'm adopted?"

"We love you just the same," the only mother Tessa had ever known told her. "Maybe more. Just kidding… You're *not* adopted. You see, it's just that you weren't born on Earth."

Relieved, Tessa laughed. "Wait. What do you mean, I wasn't born on Earth?"

"Where do you think you got your tesseracting ability?" Skye said.

"Well, I thought it was a flowery way of saying that I could 'All Things Understand,'" Tessa said, suddenly less sure of herself than ever.

"None of the witches on Earth have ever been able to tesseract," Skye said.

"Oh, for goddess's sake," Tessa said, inexplicably feeling herself threatened. She gave a short squeak, and the book vanished.

"Which is not to say that no other witches *anywhere* have been able to tesseract. I grew up on a planet called GlieseCc. Some of the female witches there could tesseract dimensions. I moved to Earth for school and later married your father. When we were expecting you, we didn't even think about tesseracting, since I don't have the knack myself. But you came early. Maybe it was the different environment, or maybe you just took after someone on my side of the family and inherited the tesseracting ability. I'll tell you, it was touch and go when you were born. People kept popping in and out, and you were too young to control your impulses. We thought it was funny, at first."

"But I still don't understand," Tessa said. "How did you get to this planet? How far is it from Earth? Can I go there?"

"Slow down," Skye said. "I'll try to explain. Although I have to say that you still don't have full control of your abilities, and I don't know if you ever will. I think the only way to really understand it is to see where you came from, in person."

"Hell, yes," Tessa said hotly.

"Language, dear. I'll think about how to make the trip tomorrow."

Tessa lay in bed, unable to sleep. Her eyes felt scratchy, and closing them didn't help. They'd felt red and irritated ever since she'd gotten a dose of black goo in the face from an exploding mo-ball. That, plus the tantalizing fact that her mother had imparted today caused her to toss and turn, looking for a more comfortable position. Her traitorous pillow had suddenly become lumpy and hard, further obstructing sleep and making her face ache. The rumbling of the house furnace was louder than usual.

Tessa'd always known she was an outsider. She was a witch, after all. But she wondered if all witches worried about being outsiders. Surely some were proud of their powers, or at least they had come to terms with them and used them to do good or to help the family. Just as that was beginning to happen with Tessa, she'd been told she was an alien from outer space. Her mother too. Tessa's mind raced, trying to remember if Mom had ever acted stranger than everyone else. She couldn't think of anything out of place. In fact, her mother was always sweet, encouraging, and a damn good cook. An ideal mom. Tessa smiled a bit, now understanding why her mother had never been one of the Twelve All in Dread. When the sun crept into her apartment and woke her, she realized she had dropped off to sleep.

Rolling out of bed, she climbed the stairs to the kitchen, to find her mother busily cooking breakfast and humming a tune about pixies and fairies, imaginary creatures that filled the legends of the people of the North.

"What about some eggs, dear?" Skye asked. "I've got blackbird and robin eggs, but we're out of chicken."

"Um, sure," Tessa said, scrutinizing her mother harder than she had in ages. Nope, she looked the same as normal.

Her mother dropped a plate of scramblets and tubers on the table. Tessa riffled through a drawer for a fork and sat down.

"Mom, am I human?" Tessa asked.

Skye started to reply, but was interrupted by the appearance of the tesseracted binder, which popped out of the air, slammed in front of Tessa, and fell open.

"It's all right in there, dear. You'll be fine—really."

Tessa regarded the notebook, her heart sinking at the prospect of wading through the thick tome for answers. Besides, that burning sensation had rekindled in her eyes. "You promised to tell me, Mom."

"I know, but it would be better if we do it after dark. You've got class today, right? Why don't we do it after dinner?"

Tessa toyed with her eggs and finished her breakfast, but she knew this was going to be the longest day in her life…

Just as she had predicted, the day crept by. Her thamaturgical economics students asked a lot of dumb questions, much to her chagrin. Professor Frakulus had told her to always say, "there's no such thing as a dumb question," when dealing with students, but he was so wrong. For example, that numbskull Finlay Etherium kept asking why the Geltrangg currency wasn't being replaced by what he considered to be a better choice based on instantaneous cryptographic transactions. As Tessa pointed out, such currencies were merely fiction. She advised everyone to save their Geltranggs if they ever wanted to get out of living with their parents. She also pointed out that Gelts were legal tender everywhere, not only here in the North. She'd proven that when visiting Scotland. Finally, the Dreadfull Bell tolled, and she gratefully excused her charges.

The sun was low in the sky when she arrived home. Of course it had been low in the sky all day, as it was winter. Nonetheless, it *was* about to set, if only for a few hours. Tessa was anxious to grab her chance to hear "the talk" that Skye had promised.

"I told your father to give us some space," Skye said. "He knows what I'm about to say, but he's giving me a chance to explain yet again why I've been reticent."

"Don't be reticent, Mom," Tessa said, a little too loudly. "Everyone respects you, and you're much too modest all the time."

"Yes, well… Let's go out back, shall we? I always feel better in the fresh air. My parents named me Skye for a reason, I guess. As I told you, you were born far away." She pointed at the darkening sky as a sprinkling of stars gradually began to spread above them.

"See the constellation that looks like a big box? It's called Scorpius. One of the stars—the biggest one—is actually multiple stars that appear to be one at this distance. The one we're from is called Gliese 667 with a capital C. The third planet out is Gliese 667Cc."

"How did you ever get to Earth from there, Mom?"

"Our civilization is quite advanced. When I married your father, I brought along a lot of advanced technology, such as the freightflinger and the mo-ball."

"So you're not really a witch?" Tessa asked.

"*Au contraire,* dear. I am most definitely a witch, just not the old-fashioned Satan-worshipping kind. More of an exchange student visiting other magic worshippers.

We had noted that a wise Earth mage had claimed that any sufficient technology is indistinguishable from magic. He was correct."

"But that star's got to be light-years away," Tessa objected. "Dad says faster-than-light-travel is impossible." She was beginning to understand that not everything her father told her was strictly true.

"Twenty-two light-years, actually. I wasn't going to stay here originally," Skye continued. "But then I met your father, and he swept me off my feet. He was terribly intelligent, with an impressive ability to make do with primitive technologies. He also had keen emotional insight. He caught me gazing longingly at the daytime sky, and brought out a telescope that night. He explained that it could resolve multiple stars. Of course, I already knew where to look.

"Later, I showed him how the freightflinger works. I thought it was kind of a funny joke at first to tell him that we could go around the galaxy in eighty days."

Tessa squinted. "I think I can see it, Mom, what's it called, Gleese? How's that possible?"

"We've got rather keen eyesight. That's another technology advance our people have. Since humans have rather delicate eyes, all citizens who plan to travel from Gliese are required to have a neuromodulation device implanted. It protects against blindness and sight impairment in the case of accidents or radiation. It also gives us the ability to see in the infrared spectrum."

Tessa gazed at the night sky, taking a lot of it in for the first time. Suddenly those twinkly lights were more than just decoration. There were real people out there. She asked her mother if they could visit GlieseCc.

"We'd have to ask your father," Skye said.

"Mom, I know he's your husband, but you don't have to ask his permission."

"It's not that, dear. He's been there before, and the journey takes a very long time. There's no guarantee everything would be as we left it after 40-plus years away."

"Oh, I see. Would we all be ancient when we got there?"

"There's some time dilation for the traveler that helps defray one's apparent time passage, but even with that, your father had to make some sacrifices when he went to GlieseCc. You and I have superior genetic heritage, but with Cornelius we had to enter into what some might call a demonic contract to keep him from aging."

"Contract? Does this involve Marmion Industries by any chance? That's their mission, right, to get out of unbreakable contracts?" Tessa had been working for G. R. Penrus, head of Marmion. Now she had a clue how she had received a job offer from them, thanks to her mother and her sister Morgana.

"Yes, good deduction. You're really quite smart, Tessa, you take after me," Skye said with a wink. "Penrus was instrumental in restoring Cornelius's youth. Fortunately he knew about a loophole to the eternal sensual fulfillment promised in the contract. He was able to remove 99% of the curse."

Tessa grimaced. There was little denying that her dad was anything other than a nerd, albeit a lovable one. She could understand that he might want to sit this visit out. It also seemed to explain her father's affinity to the sulfurous compounds emanating from his laboratory.

"Is there a way Dad could stay home without selling his soul to stay alive until we returned?" Tessa asked.

"Maybe some sort of Sleeping Beauty DNA transposon-type solution would work, if Cornelius wanted," Skye said. "We had the technology a long time ago back home, but we've always preferred not to introduce advances before others were in a position to understand it. That way, they think they invented it, although in a way, they have really just reinvented it. We could modify some old, long-inactive human genes to lengthen longevity and reactivate them in your father."

Tessa realized there were other ramifications of traveling around the galaxy in 80 days. She'd have to leave her best friend Esmeralda behind. That would make her sad. She already missed Ezzy, and she hadn't even left!

Tessa knew that she had trepidations about visiting outer space. Who wouldn't? But she could tell her mother was homesick.

"Mom, I'll bet most of the Twelve would love to take a trip to see your home, not just me. Would it be all right to ask them?"

Skye agreed, and they went back inside, arm-in-arm.

👀👀👀

The mo-ball seemed to be working fine, as Tessa called each of her sisters to invite them along on what she billed as the "trip of a lifetime." She didn't quite trust the little gomboc after its earlier escape attempt, but she was trying to give it more leeway to make its own decisions. She was just getting used to the idea that mo-balls used artificial intelligence in addition to magic, and it was unclear whether AIs were going to take over the world or become humanity's best friends. Tessa wanted it to be the latter. Her sore eyes had been improving steadily, although when she looked in the mirror, she was shocked to see her eyes had taken on a reddish glow.

Even Morgana had noticed it, and she rarely looked anyone in the eye.

"What's with the glowing eyes?" she asked. "You're not impersonating a robot, are you? That would be an odd type of glamor."

"Um, no, Mom says it's just an implant that improves your vision. I can see in the infrared and the ultraviolet now."

70

Morgana smirked. "What about x-ray vision?"

Tessa remembered the time she had accidentally tesseracted into a white room and could see the bones in her feet through her shoes. And the uncomfortable feeling that there was "something in her eye" remained. She was also experiencing little flashes of light like the pixels on a tv screen, that her mother had called "floaters."

"Maybe. I'll ask her."

"Well, I hope she doesn't give you a fire-breathing implant," Morgana said. "Me and my dragons would be out of a job at Marmion."

"Little chance of me replacing a three-ton dragon in the field," Tessa said with a grin. "Are you coming with us to GlieseCc?"

"I don't think so," Morgana said. "Dad may need me, not to mention the things here on Earth that will need looking after. Besides, I understand that our alien mother can extend our lifespans, and I'm definitely up for that. Plus, it'll be interesting to see if we advance intellectually enough to catch up with the Gliese civilization."

"If I learn anything useful, I'll be sure to bring it home. Sometimes you don't know what new technology will do. It's not always good." Tessa's voice trembled a bit. "Sorry you're staying home."

Morgana hugged Tessa and whistled for her dragonets, who were still too young to fly. Tessa sighed as she watched them troop off into the forest.

Tessa and Skye waited until the line in front of the interstellar freightflinger had thinned out. The two wore backpacks, as this was not the sort of trip where you wanted your luggage to get lost. Mosttimes, the coven of the North used freightflingers for short hops and for shipping supplies. No one except The Twelve had any idea that they could be used for space travel, and only Skye knew how do it safely.

"All right, let's go," Skye said, taking Tessa's hand and leading her through the door in the tree.

As they mounted the platform, Tessa stumbled a little. "Maybe GlieseCc will have an improved brain implant or something that'll give me better visual resolution," she joked.

"Shouldn't be necessary," Skye said. "While your implant's capabilities are nothing short of miraculous, it does take some getting used to. Like you, it's capable of learning, so your vision should get better as you get more experience with it."

"No problem," Tessa said. She just hoped she didn't experience any hallucinations that would trigger a tesseract. "Um, is there travel insurance for this sort of thing?"

"'Fraid not, Fraidy Cat," Skye said. "Ready?"

She must not have waited for an answer, because Tessa's senses seemed to switch off. She couldn't see—that wasn't a bit surprising, really—she couldn't hear—nor was that. But she also couldn't smell, taste, feel the cold depths of space, or do anything sensory. She could do nothing, but somehow she knew she still existed.

Skye had told her very little about what the journey would entail, except to advise bringing warm socks, so Tessa'd made up for that with her imagination, picturing falling down a head-spinning rainbow vortex. She was grateful there was none of that, actually. If there was one thing she could ask for to improve the trip, it would be more legroom. No, just joking... But she did wish she knew when this feeling of limbo would end. As soon as that thought popped into her head, she and Skye popped into the North freightflinger terminal on GlieseCc.

"Let me get my bearings, and we'll go to my home," Skye said.

"Oh, can we take a look around first?"

"Oh, sure," Skye agreed. "But I don't think you'll see much around the port, except for some nice landscaping."

Skye was much too modest. The sky was a brilliant blue, dotted with little puffs of white cloud. People flew above their heads, some leaving the port area, and others landing in front of the freightflinger.

Exotic flowers ringed the area, marching outward in bands of red, green, blue, and violet. Tessa laughed; there was the rainbow vortex she had imagined.

"Will we use the freightflinger to get to your house?" she asked. "I'm afraid I don't have much experience flying. We've always lived within walking distance of school or the freightflinger."

"We'll fly," Skye said. "No one here will think it odd that a couple of women are flying through the sky."

"Right. We're all witches here," Tessa agreed.

Skye watched over her sleeping daughter, unable to sleep herself. Her thoughts turned back to Tesseracta's birth, the youngest of twelve sisters Skye had born on Earth. Amazingly, the child exhibited most of the magical heritage of her mother, especially with the biological implants they had installed to ensure her viability. Skye and Cornelius hoped the advent of Tesseracta's powers would enable closer relations with her relatives on GlieseCc.

But that apparently hadn't been enough for Skye's aunts. The baby was not a native of GlieseCc, much less of the North, and her father was from a backward planet known only as Earth. A meaningless name, since the ground one stood upon on *any* planet was earth.

There was also the matter of the father's deprecated religion. Evil emanated from him, evidently from some sort of unlawful enemy assistance. Skye tried to explain that it was just a way of extending Cornelius's lifespan so that he could visit. Her pleas were ignored, as the witches of GlieseCc declared Tesseracta illegitimate. They believed Tessa might carry a curse that would infect the whole civilization. They even suggested that it might be better if Tessa were "humanely" disposed of. Skye loved Cornelius, and she loved Tessa. There didn't seem to be any way out, except to return to Earth.

Now that Tessa was grown, and Cornelius's "curse" had been voided, maybe there was a chance that she could rejoin the family. Skye frowned, determined. Tesseracta was the pride of the The Twelve All in Dread, the one who was All Things Understanding, mistress of a blend of magic and technology never before equaled.

❀❀❀

Tessa stirred, stretching and yawning as she woke from a deep sleep.

"Even though the trip seemed short, it really seemed to take it out of me," she said. "What about you, Mom? Did you get any rest?"

"I'm fine," Skye said, struggling to put on a smile. "Come on, we've got a big day ahead of us. I really want to show you the jungles of GlieseCc. The flowers are amazing viewed in full spectrum. I know your sisters will be pleased to hear about the horticultural products. It would make potions a lot easier to concoct, and they would be more effective than what we've been using at home."

They stopped for a lunch of assorted fruits. The melon-sized blueberries turned out to be Tessa's favorites, although they were an odd color of blue.

"Blue is a good color in fruit," Skye pointed out. "The pigment indicates a high amount of cyanins."

"What's next besides the farms?" Tessa asked. "What's the nightlife like?"

"Well, it's not exactly clubbing," Skye replied, "but there is going to be a moonlight circle dance tonight. Moon magic was invented here, and it carries with it a lot of significance in our world. And it's universal. Just as on

Earth, the moon is believed to add power to the rituals, especially love spells."

"Isn't that sort of thing what got us cast out of human society?" Tessa asked.

"Perhaps, but the concentration it enhances has been proven safe and effective, if not everyone wants to believe in it." They flew to a clearing of low-growing turf, where about a dozen ladies in pink peaked hats waited for the moon to rise. Tessa felt a bit out of place in her usual black hoodie and leggings, but Skye assured her there was no dress code. The singing and dancing had just begun, when an extraordinarily tall witch stepped forward and loomed over Skye.

"What are you doing here? I thought we told you never to return."

Ignoring her comment, Skye said, "Tesseracta, I'd like to introduce you to your Aunt Satu. Satu, this is my daughter, Tesseracta."

"You're not welcome here," Satu said, giving Skye a push.

Tessa stepped between them, attempting to soothe matters over, whatever those matters might be. Satu reached around her and began throttling Skye.

"Stop!" Tessa said, and before she could take it back, she added, "*Begone!*" Tessa's armor didn't pop on, but unfortunately, the tesseract began taking effect immediately. The tall witch's hands fell away, leaving her armless. Then her feet disappeared, causing her to lose a foot in height.

"Please, Tessa, don't kill her," Skye begged. The tesseract abruptly ceased. "Satu, we only came to make peace—to show you that Tessa is a real member of the family, and that her Earth blood is an asset, not a disgrace."

Satu appeared stunned, all color drained from her face in the pale moonlight. Without her hands, she was unable to cast a spell either to attack or defend herself.

Her companions crowded in, hands and wands raised, ready to help their friend.

"No, it's all right," Satu said, her voice cracking. "You've obviously proven yourself worthy, and I owe you an apology."

"While we wait for the tesseract to unwind, I won't be dancing for a while," Satu said. "Let's sing," she suggested. "This moon song was a hit before your mother was born, and she was born a long, long time ago."

At evening's end, Satu asked her sister, "What became of that cursed Earth boy, Cornelius?"

"We left him home," Skye said, "at his own request. You didn't exactly welcome him last time."

"What about the curse?" Satu asked.

"It was settled out of court," Tessa said.

Seemingly satisfied, Satu said, "When I'm back together, we'll go to the library and get some information about tesseracting."

"Oh, that won't be necessary," Skye said. "We've got a book at home."

"But I would like to meet someone else like me," Tessa said. "I mean, someone who can shift dimensions—and preferably, who knows how to control it."

"Didn't Skye tell you?" Satu said, shaking her head. "No one has ever been able to totally control it before. Maybe you'll be the exception. Your mother should know."

When Skye and Tessa prepared to return home, Satu gave them a flat containing a baker's dozen of potted moonflower starts. "This is for you and your sisters," she said. "And your mother. We hope you'll visit us often."

"Um, thanks," Tessa said, noting that she hadn't included Cornelius, Oh well, Dad wasn't much for gardening anyway. Besides, she thought the plants looked like ordinary morning glories.

"Lovely," Skye said, more graciously. "These bioluminescent night bloomers will add a powerful fragrance to the garden."

Arms laden with gifts, Tessa and Skye bid Satu adieu and stepped aboard the freightflinger.

Back home, Tessa was keen to tell her class all about her trip to the fantastic cosmos. Why hadn't they visited all the time? Still, it was good to be back home. She was reminded of the old proverb:

> *But this maxim mind—*
> *No place like Home*
> *For safety will you find*

She'd gained more appreciation for her students, too, with their Earth-honed talents and skills. That even included Etherium, although his fiscal theories were, to say the least, controversial. He was at least very easy on the eyes, especially in the infrared.

*****~~~~~*****

PART II.
MEDIEVAL AND MODERN FANTASIES

The Wet at the Top of the Stairs

"Clean that up, you lazy wretch!"

Dethen had heard that order one too many times. He was sick of cleaning up the messes of the knights and ladies and regretted the day his older brother had gotten him this job at the great castle in the south. The place had been a wonder of the world in its day, but it had fallen on harder times the past couple hundred years.

"I should have stayed in the village," he muttered, bringing a mop and bucket to swab at the puddle of red wine created when the tipsy Sir Gentry knocked over the Lady Millicent's goblet. "That's going to leave a stain."

Besides, he wasn't the lazy one. It was his brother Tally, who, ever since becoming pals with the young King Ganther, wouldn't deign to lift a finger, although his official position was valet, or sometimes squire, when the king couldn't find someone to saddle his horse and polish the gore off his sword. All Taliesin ever seemed to do was party with the knights in the dining hall, then return to his room to bury his nose in a book and pretend like he had magickal powers or something. That seemed highly unlikely to Dethen, although they did come from a village fabled as the birthplace of Merlin.

Returning to the quarters he shared with Tally, Dethen dumped the bucket's contents out the window and tossed it and the mop in the closet. Tally's bedside table was a pure disaster—piles of books, plates of decaying food, and assorted crucibles filled with the metals and ashes of his alchemy experiments. He'd told Deth never to touch anything, upon penalty of sibling reprisal. Still, it was hard to ignore, Deth being so tidy by nature.

His gaze fell upon the stack of books. The one at the bottom was much fancier than the others, bound in embossed leather and fastened with a clasp. Tally was obviously trying to hide it in plain sight. It looked a bit dusty, so Deth couldn't resist running his finger along the book's spine, tracing a clean path. To his surprise, the trail seemed to close itself, replacing the dust he'd removed. He tried it several times. Sometimes he got stuck trying things over and over again. It was kind of a tic, Tally had said. Deth just called it "being thorough." No luck. This book stubbornly stayed dusty.

The wooden door creaked as Tally returned. Deth jumped back and busied himself neatly stacking the wood alongside the fireplace.

"Hah, did you see Millicent making a fool of herself tonight?" Tally said jovially.

"How could I miss it? Sir Gentry was all over her, literally," Deth agreed. Mostly, he couldn't see the attraction. Millicent was amply endowed, but she was loud and vulgar. But she *was* amply endowed…

Deth crawled into bed and pulled his blanket over his face. He was learning to sleep through the sulfurous and other smells generated in Tally's nightly researches. More than once he'd awakened screaming hoarsely, his heart pounding in panic for fear of perishing in a fire. Now, if he could just ignore the occasional "whomp" sound, like air rushing into an explosion, he'd have it made. Every time he peeked, however, there was nothing to see. Finally he drifted off, hoping he'd dream about his childhood days in the village. His mother had once promised him a puppy of his own, but that probably wouldn't happen, now that he worked in the castle.

The next morning Deth awoke to the cock's crow. At least something here reminded him of home, even if it was at an ungodly hour. He sprang out of bed and hurried over to the fireplace to coax the embers back into a small blaze and clear the brimstone smell. Tally continued to snore gently; he wouldn't be up before noon. Deth pulled on a homespun cape and prepared to go downstairs to help with the general chores of rousing the castle. He stopped, turning once again toward Tally.

"Tally?" he called. "Tally!" more urgently this time.

"Wha— What is it?" Tally sat up and rubbed his eyes.

"Would you teach me to read sometime?"

"Sure, whatever you want. Just go and leave me in peace," Tally replied. He flopped back down, instantly asleep.

Deth pestered Tally unceasingly until he made good on his promise, and the reading lessons began in earnest.

"What's this word?" Tally prompted.

"Un—, un—," Deth began.

"Unspeakable," Tally finished for him. The 'un' part means 'not.'"

"So, that must be why they call the ladies' undergarments 'un-mentionables,'" Deth opined. Tally smirked.

"You're really making progress," Tally said later. "Maybe I'll teach you to write too, and you can write letters for the ladies."

Deth smiled and said that sounded pleasant. He would carefully bide his time before asking to take notes for Tally, or even to take a look at the fancy book. No need to upset him un-necessarily. Dethen complimented himself silently at his expert usage of the 'un'-word.

The lessons came to an abrupt halt when the summer tournament season rolled around. One of Tally's official duties was the rubbing of sheep's fat into the king's stirrups and scabbards, although he palmed this task off to Deth whenever possible.

Deth too was busier than usual, delivering notes from ladies to their champions and fetching bits of silk for them to embroider as battle favors. Deth knocked on the door to Lady Millicent's rooms, but the only answer was a peal of laughter as the ladies joked about who had the greater chance of winning. Millicent's companion, the homely but really quite nice Lady Valerane, bit her lip and concentrated on her needlework. Although Deth was just a boy, he knew the ladies were really discussing who had the bigger. . .

"Eeek!" Millicent yelped. "Who said you could come in, you little rat?"

"I knocked, m'lady. I've brought the bolts of silk you wanted."

"Well, you took long enough. Put them down and get out. Go get us some tea, and don't let it get cold this time."

The Wet at the Top of the Stairs

That afternoon, Deth went to his room to take a breather. The ladies would be getting ready for dinner, and heaven only knew what Tally was up to lately.

It was nice to be without supervision for a change, Deth thought, edging slightly closer to the book on the table. Almost without his bidding, his hand shot out and pulled the tome out from under the others in Tally's disordered pile.

Glancing about, he pulled it against his chest. Hurrying over to his cot, he sat down, already fumbling to open the clasp. A musty odor wafted up as he opened the book, which appeared to be an old French grammaire. Just his lot. He could read now, but the language wasn't Brythonic. The frontispiece featured a drawing of an angry-looking man, and someone had scrawled a caption.

He could make out a few French words, "Arabe," and "fou." So this person was a mad Arab? That didn't make any sense. The only Arab he had ever seen was at last season's tournaments. Come to think of it, Tally had followed the Saracen around like a dog. What was his name? Omar. Yes, that was it. But he was a warrior and bore no resemblance to this evil-looking character depicted in the book. Was he the owner, and was this a warning not to steal the book?

Deth noticed his eyes were beginning to burn. This castle was often smoky, and it could be a chore trying to read a book by candlelight. Suddenly the words on the page flared as the letters traced in flame. That's more like it, he thought. He began to leaf through the pages, his excitement growing at what seemed to be a magical bond with the book.

Maybe he could understand the French words a little better if he sounded them out.

Ça n'est pas mort qui peut dormir éternellement
Et avec les éternités étrange la mort-même peut mourir

That didn't sound quite right. He tried again.

La mort-même peut mourir

Better, but not quite. He was going to repeat it until he got it perfect.

LA MORT-MÊME PEUT MOURIR

Deth's words boomed out as though projected from the deep, dark dungeon below his feet. He slammed the book closed, extinguishing the light and struggling not to break wind. Marshalling his senses, he noticed that the sun was setting, and shakily replaced the book at the bottom of the pile. Then he hurried down to the dining hall to help with the opening night banquet the king was hosting for the tournament.

The hall bustled, as servants scurried about, dragging a dozen trestle tables from storage behind the cavernous kitchens and arranging them in a big open rectangle. The famous round table was spacious, but it would not accommodate the fifty warriors assembled for the festival. Deth staggered under a load of straw, with orders to lay an even coating on the stone floor. It did make cleanup easier; the greasy bones and raw garbage tossed by the diners could just be swept out with the straw.

Finally all was in readiness, as the parade of knights and ladies entered the great hall and took their seats. Servers circuited the table, keeping the flagons at the full. Deth took his customary post in the corner, sitting on the floor with his hands clasped around his knees so as not to trip any of the waiters. A harpist plucked out the haunting melodies of Ys, the mythical fairyland.

The room hushed as Lady Millicent entered the room. She was undeniably a vision, in a rustling green silk dress embellished with gold threads. Sir Randolph of Auron handed her to the table, over the scowling disapproval of the fat Sir Gentry. Then Millicent broke the spell by opening her mouth.

"Are we now allowing the rats into the hall?" she shrilled, pointing at Deth in his dim corner. Sir Gentry's squire grabbed Deth by the arm and expelled him unceremoniously.

Although still stinging from the insult, Deth waited outside until the last guest left so he could start the cleanup.

"That un-civil Millicent! I'll see she pays for her cocky attitude," Deth mumbled, sweeping the detritus on the floor into a big pile. The area was scattered with peelings from an exotic fruit Sir Omar had brought as a present from Moorish Iberia, and Deth nearly lost his balance more than once when he accidentally stepped on one of the slippery jackets. "I'll fix her—I'll put this stinking rubbish at the top of the stairs outside her room," he said, eyeing the results of his odious task with satisfaction.

Revenge properly executed, Deth returned to his room and fell unconscious onto his cot.

The next morning, a scream rang through the castle from the rooms above. Deth opened his eyes, saw Tally sleeping through the uproar as usual, and ran out toward the stairs. Evidently Lady Millicent had discovered the pile, he thought with satisfaction. Wiping the grin off his face, he feigned a look of concern as he loped up the curved stone staircase. It was still dark at the top, but he was familiar with the number of steps. As he rounded the final bit, he spied the wet pile of garbage—and it was moving.

A number of what looked like tentacles wiggled from under the fetid pile, dragging it toward the stairs. Deth was shocked. He'd never seen food scraps go bad so fast, and the worms were un-comprehensibly large.

He swallowed. "You screamed, m'Lady?"

"It wasn't me, you dolt. That was the King. This is all your doing! The thing tried to eat my foot," Millicent wailed. She showed her foot, which was no longer dainty and was dripping blood. She was going to have a limp, that was sure.

Deth shrank against the wall as the straw pile oozed down the staircase. He considered comforting Millicent, but seeing her blotchy face thought better of it, instead cautiously pursuing the thing, whatever it was. It left an un-mistakable trail of vitriolic slime that was not hard to follow. As he looked ahead, he saw that it had stopped in front of Tally's and his room!

"Tally! Look out! The garbage has been magicked!" Deth cried.

The door opened. Tally yawned, pulling on his night shirt. He espied the slime trail leading to the room and quickly slammed the door shut.

The door opened again, and Tally held the book. He began chanting something, and the pile did an abrupt about-face and fled down the next course of stairs.

Tally looked at Deth. "Did you have something to do with this?"

"Me? No!" Deth said. "I think."

"Have you been touching my books?"

"No! Well, only a little," Deth admitted.

"Did you say anything from this one?" he said, holding up the grammaire. "Sir Omar gave it to me. I was supposed to destroy it."

"Well, I read something about 'mort,' was all. And there was something about a Welshman named Crwthor-- or was it Crwthllu? I didn't really understand anything in it."

Tally made him point to the page he had read from. The picture of the Arab was looking even more evil than he had remembered.

"I told you to keep your hands off. Anyone who tries to use this book usually comes to a bad end," Tally said. "Come on, we've got to get to the king." They tore back up the stairs, deftly avoiding the slime.

"What can the king do?" Deth asked between puffs.

"He's got a sword of power." Deth didn't know what that would do.

"Can't we just burn the pile?" he asked.

"Quite the opposite. It will probably spontaneously combust and set everything afire. We've got to stop it before it destroys the castle."

They were a bit late on that score. Myriad screams emanated from below. A quick look out of a turret slit toward the ground below revealed dozens of the piles, all flaming and crawling around on tentacles. Several knights were already dead, lying in smoldering, bleeding heaps. Although it was well into morning, the sky was still nearly black, and the earth shook.

"How did it multiply so fast?" Deth wondered aloud.

"Well, how many times did you repeat the incantation?"

Deth didn't want to say the number—it was probably un-countable.

King Ganther crouched naked and gibbering atop his malodorous mattress, which was stained yellow as a crow's foot, but we shall speak of that no further. The king came to his senses after a few well-placed slaps. Luckily he trusted Tally unquestioningly with the sword Eurandel and pointed hysterically at the tentacles trying to climb the bedpost. Tally commenced a hard day's work of beating and stabbing the piles until they went back to the unspeakable world they had come from. It is said the white-hot flames from the mouths of the two chimeras on the hilt of Eurandel blazed so bright they were dreadful to look upon. Tally descended the stairs, working systematically. Deth felt a little guilty, seeing his brother do all the work.

"Um, is there anything I can do to help?"

"I think you've done quite enough," Tally retorted, hacking and slashing at the next unutterable horror. "Oh, all right, take the scabbard and go heal Lady Millicent's wounds."

Unreasonably happy, Deth dashed off.

But by that time, the whole of Castle Camelot was alight.

The king cancelled the tournament, and it was many a year before he threw another one. It's rumored he slept with Eurandel under his pillow the rest of his life. Most people tried their best to forget about King Ganther's reign and how Camelot was utterly destroyed under his unmindful watch.

*****~~~~~*****

Rage, Rage, Against the Dying of the Age

Now. Now. Now!

Valerane Duvall stared at the horizon as the last rays of the sun disappeared over the late February Somerset landscape.

Surely force of will would speed up the comet's apparition.

She shivered and wrapped her woolen cloak more tightly, stamping her feet a little to bring feeling back. Another half hour. Nothing yet. She found herself holding her breath and forced herself to exhale, marveling as tiny ice crystals condensed in the fog around her head.

Just when she thought she could stand it no longer, there it was.

A fuzzy ball, visible to the naked eye and appreciably bigger than the surrounding stars, appeared in the sky, towing a thin tail of fire. Fanfares of trumpets sounded in her mind, accompanied by the thunder of drums. Her first bona fide *omen*.

Her tutor, the King's magician Taliesin, would not approve of her being out here after dark, unaccompanied.

But at this hour Valerane's usual companion, the blonde Lady Millicent, would have garnered all the knights' attention after dinner, so it had been easy to slip out. Besides, Camelot's heyday was long past, and the tattered portcullis leaked people like a sieve.

During Val's morning sorcery lessons, Tally consulted his books, which he kept under lock and key, and showed her the prediction about the comet's appearance.

"It has appeared in the heavens every 70 years for at least a millennium," Taliesin said. "The comet will probably not be impressive enough to revive King Ganther's reputation, which has lately fallen upon hard times, but it has often presaged important events of some sort. King Arthur himself was crowned during one such occasion."

Val decided right then that she would be there to greet the comet in person. She felt in her pocket for her crystal, the last keepsake she had of her family. With a pang, she thought of her twin sister Ivonne, who had been shipped across the Channel with her parents in order to secure some godforsaken plot of land in Normandy that the King felt entitled to. Val stayed behind as insurance that the family would remain loyal to King Ganther.

A small crack or imperfection in the crystal she hadn't noticed before began to phosphoresce faintly. Upon closer examination, she saw that it was a twin of the comet. With a pang, she thought of her long-lost twin, who had been shipped across the Channel with her parents in order to secure some godforsaken plot of land in Normandy that the King felt entitled to. Val stayed behind as insurance that the family would remain loyal to King Ganther. She'd never felt at home here. Though she was handsome enough, her Gallic, aquiline nose and jet-black hair betrayed the fact that she was not a Saxon native.

Perhaps this was the omen she sought—that she and her twin would be reunited.

Shaking herself out of her reverie, Val reached into the front of her gown and pulled the hidden talisman from a small leather bag hung on a chain around her neck. She held the crystal, which appeared to be an ordinary chunk of quartz, up toward the comet and waited.

A snap of twigs and raucous male voices interrupted the silence. Val flipped up her hood and jumped behind a nearby tree as a troop of armed ruffians hove into view. Though there was much clanking, they were not wearing armor, just leather breastplates. The leader wore a helmet with demon horns. They looked mangy and half-starved. *Vikings!*

She'd heard rumors about these Northmen, who had discovered a way to sail across the ocean and raid along the English coast. What were they doing this far south? She glanced at the place where she had been standing and hoped they wouldn't spot her footprints in the snow. Only after they were nearly out of sight did one of them turn to glance backward, his kohl-rimmed eyes sweeping across the tree she hid behind.

She had to get back to the castle and impart the bad news to the king and his small coterie of knights. The Saxons did their best to protect the lands hereabout, but incursions from Celts from the north and now Vikings were taking their toll, and they were stretched thin. At least this time they would get some warning. She knew a shortcut through these woods and would arrive at the castle well ahead of the raiders, who would have to negotiate the traps set for the unwary along the road. She wondered briefly why they had ventured inland across Dorset, when there were easier pickings on the coast.

Val pounded on Tally's door. He was a heavy sleeper. Finally, the door opened a crack.

"What?" he asked groggy.

"There's a group of Viking raiders headed this way!" Val said in a hoarse whisper.

Taliesin pulled on a surcoat and came into the hall, not forgetting to lock his door. "I'll inform the king," he said.

"Can I help?"

"No, you must prepare the ladies to head for the secret sanctuary."

Val would have preferred to help inform the king, but she nodded and traveled down the hall toward her and Millicent's quarters. She didn't want to have to explain how she knew raiders were coming. She was just glad he believed her.

Soon the klaxon of bells reverberated throughout the compound. Residents hurried through the halls, gathering weapons and wiping sleep from their eyes.

Millicent ran her fingers through her flaxen hair and wailed, "What should I wear? What should I take?"

Val didn't know. What do you take to a siege? Shifting a loaf of bread she had grabbed from the kitchen to her left hand, she put her arm around Millicent's shoulders, and hustled her best friend to the brick wall hiding the sanctuary. She reached down to a particular brick at knee level and pushed on it. A narrow panel sprang out slightly, affording just enough room for a person to enter sideways. The door would be the only way in or out, and might be defensible with spear and sword.

"Get in here," she said, handing the bread to Millicent.

"But, aren't you coming?" Millicent asked, lower lip trembling. Val regarded the beautiful Millicent, beloved by all the knights but, sadly, lacking the sense of a chicken.

"I'll try to get back soon, Milli. There's something I've got to do. Don't let anyone in, unless you hear three blasts." Val was justly proud of her ability to emit ear-splitting whistles.

"Don't we get a knight—?" Milli started to say before the door slammed.

Val made her way toward the King's quarters. There she found two guards stationed outside the door.

"Is Taliesin here? Or the King?"

Sir Gentry, a chubby and self-important knight, had taken it upon himself to protect the king's quarters, and was not very helpful.

"You might try the west wall, m'Lady," he said.

She curtsied, and ran off to the west staircase. She raised her skirt and ascended the curved stairs two at a time. She wanted to find out if the King had the Sword of Power with him. That was their only chance. Eurandel had been decisive in repelling the recent invasion by unspeakable magick creatures from another realm. That and Taliesin's skill, of course.

Val scanned the defenders atop the west wall. Some soldiers were heating a vat of oil to be poured on invaders at the gate. The trebuchet stood abandoned, with no one to man it. *That would be a sight*, Val thought, *a couple of fireballs blazing like comets out upon the enemy. . .* But she saw no Taliesin, and no King. Had they left without her? Looking to the west, she noticed the glow of fire. Now she knew the reason for the Vikings' boldness: they had set fire to the King's last two ships before heading for the castle. It appeared there would be no escape seaward. Guilty, she realized that if her thoughts hadn't been so faraway with the comet, she might have noticed much earlier. So… not her twin sister, then.

It was over pretty quickly. Myriad screams emanated from below. Val turned and looked down into the courtyard to see that several knights were already dead, lying in various degrees of disarrangement and oozing blood or missing limbs. Gasping involuntarily at the gruesome sight, she began running toward the staircase and had almost made it when an iron grip caught her arm and spun her around.

A lumbering giant of a man with long, filthy braids and brilliant blue eyes grinned at her. She screamed and felt herself lifted off the ground as he tossed her over his shoulder and loped off, waving a heavy broad blade. He continued to the west wall, where she had been standing moments earlier, and set her down long enough to dispatch the rest of the castle defenders. He then turned back to where she crouched in terror and flung her back over his shoulder. She felt the blood rush to her head, and all was blackness.

Valerane awoke in the smoke-filled courtyard, surrounded by crying women, as raiders rounded up slaves to be sent home. A knot of warriors stood off to the side. The huge raider who had captured Val nudged the leader, pointing toward her direction with his hatchet. *What did they want with her?* He signaled to his men to take a break from killing everyone in sight.

"Lady," the leader called, "where is your king?"

She stared at him. Dirty as the rest of his band, he was nonetheless tall and straight, and looked of noble bearing.

"He has escaped," Valerane managed to squeak, wide-eyed.

"Lucky for him," the chieftain said, laughing. His men laughed with him. "Then it looks like he's left us a new home and plenty of women to feed us." He winked at her. She had an idea what that meant. She expected to be bent over a table at any moment and divested of her virginity.

She heard a high-pitched shriek and turned her head. A raider was dragging a struggling prisoner into the courtyard. Lady Millicent! Val cursed under her breath. Milli should have stayed in the sanctuary and waited until Val found a way to get to her and spirit them both away.

The leader walked over to Milli and introduced himself as Bolli. He asked her name and then repeated the same question he'd asked Val:

"Lady Millicent, where is your king?" Of course, Millicent had no idea. "I will question you further in the morning," Bolli said, his gaze lingering on the rents in Milli's gown that revealed her ample charms. Milli ran over to Val, where they clung to each other.

Bolli ordered the ladies locked in the dungeons, while the few remaining servants were put to work feeding his hungry troops. *They must be hungry indeed to pass up pillaging and ravaging for food,* Val thought gratefully.

In the near-darkness of the dungeon, illuminated only by a guttering torch, Valerane thought about the day's dismal events. She hadn't seen either the king or Tally and wondered if they were together. Where would they go? She had a good guess. She needed an escape plan to enable her to find the king and bring him back with reinforcements to retake the castle, what was left of it. As long as he had Eurandel, Ganther would be the rightful king—it wouldn't do to have Vikings running things. They were ignorant pagans, believing in old gods and unlearned in even the simplest ways of magick.

Valerane shut out the sounds of laughter and feasting above and the gentle sound of Milli snoring beside her and took out her crystal. The comet within it began to pulse, and pictures began to take shape. The Viking leader, Bolli, sat atop a horse surveying from a hill as his men burned the countryside and cut villagers into pieces. She couldn't tell if she was seeing the future of England near or far, yet she knew Bolli was key to her strategy. She saw him take the hand of a woman with love in his eyes. The woman was not her—it was Millicent. *I should have known*, Val thought, a little green-eyed.

Val knew now what to do. She would ensorcel Bolli to be more powerfully drawn to her friend, merely speeding the proper course of events. Emerging from her vision, she reached for the torch and burned off a lock of Milli's hair, fanning the smoke and watching it seep away under the door. Val chanted quietly, reciting the attraction spells that Taliesin had taught her. When she was finished, she replaced the talisman under her gown. It felt warm. She pulled her cape around herself and fell into an uneasy sleep.

After an evening depleting the king's excellent wine stores, Bolli excused himself from the dining hall and headed for the king's bedroom. There he unstrapped his sword and hopped into the tall four-poster bed to settle comfortably in the down cushions. He blew out the candle and soon fell into a deep sleep. A faint yellow-gray vapor flowed under his door, along the floor, and up onto the bed, where it took the shape of a golden-haired maiden. "Bolli, my Bolli," the woman of his dreams whispered, lying down and pressing herself against him.

At dawn, a servant brought a breakfast of bread and oatcakes for the ladies. To his surprise, there was already a Viking in the cell, along with Lady Millicent. He set the tray on the floor and made to leave.

"One moment," the Viking said. "I was just leaving too." The two left the cell, while Millicent stared.

Once outside the dungeon, the Viking headed for the courtyard, his hood obscuring his face. He saddled a fine grey horse that had belonged to Lady Millicent and rode out the castle gate unremarked.

When she was sure no one was following, Valerane resumed her normal aspect. It had been no problem tricking suggestible people and making her exit. She smiled to herself, confident of her powers and envisioning her future as the greatest of sorceresses. She'd never dared range so far from the castle, even if she could, for fear of bringing retribution upon her family, but now she was on a quest to find the King. She had a guess where he might be.

She rode much of the day, until she came to a Christian abbey, inhabited by a sect of brown-robed monks. A parish cemetery stretched off to the side, and a funeral was in progress. The monk pronouncing the service eyed her royal clothing and called, "My Lady, would you do us the honor of joining us?"

That suited Val fine. She had hoped to ask the monks for some food and perhaps a place to rest for the night. She dismounted and went to the front of the small crowd to stand alongside the abbot. The grave was for a small child, a girl named Mary. It was wrenching to see the poor mother, who had probably fought a losing battle to keep life from slowly deserting her child. Val wondered whether if she had been there early enough she might have supplied medicaments. This looked like the children's section of the graveyard. Val scanned the inscriptions on the headstones of the little ones who had died before their time. One even stretched back as far as fifteen years. Suddenly she focused. The name on that stone said "Duvall." She looked more closely at the date. It was very close to the date her family had left Somerset. The monk crossed himself to end the service and began leading the mourners away toward the abbey. She turned to follow them in, determined to ask about the grave.

"Yes, lady, I remember it well," the abbot said over supper. "It was the infant daughter of Lady Catherine and Sir Guillaume Duvall. A tragedy, because they had two other girls, a rare case of triplets. Unfortunately, the smallest never took a breath and died immediately at birth."

"What was her name?" Val asked. After dinner he consulted the record book. His finger pointed to the entry.

"Evagel Duvall. We weren't going to give her a name, since she wasn't baptized, but Lady Catherine insisted."

"I believe she was my sister, Father," Valerane said. "I never knew she existed."

"Ah, perhaps it was God's will that you come here and learn of her," the monk suggested. Val was too tactful to say it was probably just a depressing coincidence. That night the oblivion of sleep again eluded her. She walked outside and stared at the comet, which continued to burn in the sky.

Val set out again the next morning, leaving a small donation in the abbey's poorbox. It was beginning to snow again, and none of the monks saw her depart. Soon her tracks were no longer to be seen. She continued northwest, toward Wales.

She sought the village of Carmarthen, said to be Merlin's birthplace hundreds of years ago. She couldn't ask directions, since she had a hunch that Taliesin and King Ganther were headed for the same destination in secret. Soon she was hopelessly lost, and spent several days going in ever larger circles. She felt weighed down by the news of her dead sister and began to doubt that she would ever be a great sorceress when she couldn't even find her way without getting lost. Perhaps it was time to put aside her girlish fancy of twin omens.

Finally, the cloud cover cleared up enough so that she could see the night sky. There was the north star, and reassuringly, there was the comet, practically motionless its tail seeming to point her way.

At length she stumbled upon the settlement of Carmarthen and stopped on a hill above the town to see if she could recognize any of the inhabitants. Her horse moved nervously, and she looked behind to see a teenage boy gathering wood and humming to himself.

"That's six," said the boy Dethen. "Seven, eight, oh… hello, my Lady. Wait, I've seen that horse before. It belongs to Lady Millicent. Do you know her?" he asked, looking hopeful.

"Indeed I do," Val replied. "You must be Dethen."

"Yes," he answered, amazed that she knew who he was. "Are you here to see Tally?"

"Yes, please." It was all easier than she thought. No sorcery required. This was Tally's little brother, and the reason for all the locks and keys.

Deth kept picking up sticks and counting them as they worked their way back to the town. *Odd boy*, Val thought. After a while, Val reached down and boosted him onto the horse behind her. Time was of the essence, after all.

Taliesin didn't appear to be totally surprised to see her. She never knew if he had foresight or was just a good judge of character.

"What led you here?" he asked.

"I remembered when you described your home here in Wales, and—I just followed the comet."

Taliesin grunted and pulled on her horse's bridle, bringing them around to the back of his cottage. There, King Ganther sat on a chair of rough branches softened by a fur pelt, sharpening Eurandel with a whetstone.

"Ah, the young lady, Valerane, is it?"

You know very well who I am, she thought. *You took me from my parents.*

"My Lord," she said, kneeling.

"Arise, my dear. Tell me what news you have of the castle."

"It is in the hands of the Vikings, Sire. I've come to seek you to bring soldiers to take it back."

"Hmm... Well, I don't know if I can do that," the King demurred. "I'm just the one person, you see." *He really is a bit dim*, Val thought. She looked over at Tally, who looked none too pleased with her proposition.

"Well, I've heard that Merlin might be sleeping in a tree somewhere around here. Could he help us? He brought King Arthur to power, you know."

"We're all Christians, here, girl, and that's just a myth," the King said. Tally cleared his throat.

"Perhaps not, Lord. My family has kept information about the whereabouts of the supposed tree, and it has been said by the locals that they have occasionally encountered a hamadryad. Whether that would be Merlin, I can't say, but we could investigate, if you will permit it."

The King slid Eurandel back into its sheath and nodded. "Nothing ventured, nothing gained," he said gamely.

"Can I come?" Dethen said. "Merlin's my howevermany great grandfather, too."

Never without his potions, keys, and books, Taliesin gathered them into a leather bag and led the way out of the village and up the hill.

There was only the one hill, there beingt very few high spots around these parts.

"There." Tally pointed to a stand of poplars. The ground was soggy, and the snow was beginning to thaw, but they managed to slog over and breach the small thicket in front of it. As they advanced, the poplars gave way to oaks, and the sky began to darken, though it was midday. The caw of a rook broke an unnatural silence.

Val reached up and pulled off several lengths of mistletoe dangling from the lower branches of the oaks and fashioned them into necklaces for each of them.

"Protection against witchcraft," she said. "In case we encounter the unexpected."

"But aren't *we* the witches?" Dethen asked. Taliesin laughed, and said, "He's got a point. I've taught you well, I see." He pointed to one of the largest trunks. "This one, I think." He set down his bag in front of a big oak that looked like it had been blasted by lightning.

"Merlin!" he called. "Show yourself if you will."

Val, who like the King had half believed that Merlin was only a myth in spite of her sorcery training, was astounded when a wizened creature appeared. He was dark brown, the color of the tree trunk, and was nearly invisible, except for the brilliant whiteness of his eyes encircling a pair of leaf-green irises.

"What do you want, boy?" the creature asked. "And why do you bring the evil sorceress Morgana? It is she who imprisoned me here."

Val looked at Tally. *A little help, here?*

"Grandfather, this is not Morgana, though she is a witch like us. We seek your aid in bringing King Arthur's grandson Ganther back to his rightful place."

The creature studied Ganther. "He's nothing like Arthur," he sniffed. "But wait, what is that at your waist?"

Ganther said, "What? You mean Eurandel—my sword?"

"If it is your sword, you are the king," Merlin said. "Would you give me it?" He looked greedily at the two chimeras on the hilt, said to be able to shoot flames from their mouths so bright that they were dreadful to look upon.

"Grandfather," Tally wheedled, "you couldn't wield Eurandel. And anyway, you are bound to this tree for eternity. Since Ganther is the true king, would you help him raise an army to regain his kingdom?"

"Well, you've got all you need already," Merlin said. "She's got that talisman thing. It'll do the trick."

"What talisman?" Tally asked Val.

"The one she wears under her dress," Merlin said. "It is the symbolic mate of the comet currently over our heads that presages the return of a great king. Or at least that is what you'll tell everyone who'll listen. You've seen the comet, I take it?"

"Of course," Tally said, looking offended. "But it is pretty unprepossessing."

"If you make a great deal of it," Merlin responded, "it should take little effort to raise an army of superstitious dolts who'll fight for you gladly."

At first they all looked doubtfully at each other, but then Ganther said, "Hell, yes, we'll do it." He turned to

Val and said, "Lady, I'm grateful to have you as my herald."

Nonplussed, Val curtsied. She wasn't used to being appreciated.

"Good, now get out of here. I'm tired," Merlin said. "And don't forget there'll be Orionids." Val and Tally both made mental notes to look that up if they ever got home.

Through the long winter, the King did his part in recruiting new troops, offering rousing speeches wherever they went and pointing to the omen in the sky. But on more than one occasion, they had to dodge marauding raiders, reminding Val of her earlier visions.

"Are you sure we can trust Merlin's advice?" she asked. "After all, he's been cooped up in a tree for centuries." Taleisin merely stated over and over his belief that Merlin could do no wrong, and that his love of Britain was enduring.

Finally, as Beltaine approached, the ranks of the king's army swelled. People were eager to retake Camelot and to celebrate the ancient spring festival of renewal and optimism. King Ganther lost no opportunity to remind them that Vikings had no such celebrations, even though they in fact did.

"It is time to teach these pagans a lesson," he said. "We must put them back in their rightful places in the North."

Taliesin agreed loudly in support of the King. "And we must put the King back in his rightful place!" The army cheered, their morale heartened by the extra venison Ganther's archers were hauling in from the forests.

Taliesin and Valerane scoured Tally's augury books for weather spells and determined that late April would provide an auspicious stretch of fair weather for the invasion.

Once again, it was over quickly. The Vikings had grown soft and inattentive, enjoying the last of the king's wine cellar and provisions. The portcullis remained in disrepair.

After a modicum of effort, his troops raised the portcullis sufficient to admit the king, and he rode into the courtyard. Luckily, most of the Viking horde was out raiding, and the few remaining defenders were rounded up. Two of those were Bolli, and his new wife Millicent, surprised to see their reign cut short.

The King decreed that Bolli must die for daring to attack Camelot. Milli threw herself at the king's feet and begged him to spare Bolli.

Val knew that Milli had played a role in distracting Bolli from his tendencies toward pillaging and noted that she had actually improved the housekeeping within the castle. In particular, she had very neatly stacked all of the gold and silver in one room, along with bolts of silk to be packed for shipment back to Iceland.

Valerane whispered something to the King, and he turned to Bolli.

"The Lady Valerane has asked that you be tried by Eurandel," he pronounced. Bolli was obviously afraid but stood his ground as the king pointed the tip of the blade at his heart. The chimeras on the hilt began to glow, and Bolli closed his eyes, preparing to be incinerated by fire.

Instead, the twin streams of fire parted, missing Bolli and blasting chunks out of the courtyard wall on either side. Totally blinded, the onlookers waited for their vision to return to see what was left of Bolli. To everyone's dismay, he was unharmed.

"Eurandel has pronounced Bolli worthy," Valerane intoned. The king looked dubious, but he had no choice but to agree with her pronouncement. Val suggested that the king send Bolli and Milli back to Iceland with a small treasure to preserve their dignity.

"It has been foretold that Bolli will be a civilizing influence on the Northmen," Val said. She further interceded so that there would be no bloody reprisal for Bolli's men.

"Thank you, Lady Valerane," Bolli said. "I am in your debt. If I can do anything for you…"

"You've just got to stop killing everyone you meet," Val interrupted, to scattered laughter.

Milli waved her signature green silk kerchief tearfully as she and her husband took leave of the only home and few friends she had ever known. Val smiled, picturing Milli stuffing Iceland's women into the latest fashions. She pitied the poor unfortunate who ended up being Lady Millicent's maidservant.

In gratitude for her service in restoring Camelot, King Ganther gave Val her own castle along the sea near Westeress. He also granted her further request. She and Taliesin stood on the beach to greet her family in person when they crossed the Channel from Normandy. Her mother Catherine cried and reached out to stroke her hair.

"You look so much like your sister." Ivonne stepped shyly from behind their mother. After she and Val embraced, Ivonne asked, "Who have you brought with you?"

"This is my mentor, the great sorcerer Taliesin," Val said proudly.

"The Lady Valerane is too modest," Tally said. "She knows more than I do now."

It was clear that some sort of spark passed between Tally and Ivonne, for soon they were talking happily to the exclusion of all others. Val thought it strange, for there was no such attraction between her and Tally, although she and her sister were as alike as stars in the sky. Ivonne had the same dark hair and aquiline nose, yet perhaps there was an extra brightness in her eyes. By summer's end, Ivonne had agreed to accompany Taliesin to his home in Wales and become his wife. He even gave her a key to the cottage. Val snorted. He had never trusted her or Dethen with the key to anything. It was hard to imagine him settling down.

As she bade the sister she had yearned for a bittersweet goodbye, she remembered that the comet had passed, and its purpose had been fulfilled. Val mused on the meaning of it all. Was there ever really an omen? Had her struggle to become a sorceress been worth it? She and Tally used to want to be famous; why had that changed? Maybe they both recognized that time changes everything, and even fame was fleeting compared with the beauty and intensity of life.

Valerane couldn't see much hope for a less violent world without the resort of magick, yet she felt that magick's days were numbered. At least the king's sword had bought the kingdom a little time.

She took a last walk under the night sky. The crisp scent of approaching winter filled Val's nostrils. A shower of baleful meteors creased the firmament over Westeress, as impressive in its way as the single comet had been. She had remembered to look it up—these were the Orionids that Merlin had mentioned, said to foretell the end of an age. Another omen that would come true, she felt certain.

She would not go gentle, but she *would* go. Chanting an ancient spell, Valerance touched her talisman and rendered the castle invisible until further notice—or at least until another interesting omen came along.

They say Ganther slept with Eurandel under his pillow the rest of his life, although he didn't get to enjoy it long. The Vikings soon returned in greater numbers—at least temporarily— and Camelot passed into the mists of time.

*****〰〰〰*****

The Horrible and Terrifying Deeds of Alcofribas the Bold, Son of the Widow Althea, of Whom Little Is Known

by Jar-An Lei Wu

From nearly two leagues up, Alcofribas had a bird's-eye view of the destruction dealt by the giants rampaging across the valley near his mother's farm. Only last week it had been breathtakingly gorgeous, a veritable panorama of patchwork green and gold... to hear his brother tell it.

A low rumble shook the branch he was standing on. Hastily, he grabbed for a stray tendril.

"You won't get rid of me that easily," he muttered. He noted with regret that the sleeve of his jacket was torn. Mother had scrimped for months to afford the fine fabric.

She'd made it for him, along with the fashionable hose and parachute pants. He peered in his rucksack. Yep, it was still there. With a sigh, he resumed the long climb.

The trunk shook again, dislodging him for good this time. He landed on his back in the soft turf at the base, squashing the unfortunate creature in the rucksack. A few feathers and a sticky golden liquid oozed out from under the flap. A familiar face hovered over him, grinning in a most annoying way.

"Didn't make it, huh?" his brother Jacques said.

"Oh, shut up," Alcofribas replied. "This is all your fault anyway."

"Sorry," Jacques said. "But if you hadn't been off playing your lute at that festival, Mom wouldn't have asked me to sell the cow... and you know the rest."

Al bit his tongue. His brother "Jack" was quite adept at shrugging off mistakes and projecting them onto others.

"It was only for a week. I was trying to earn some money at a gig, which is more than I can say for you." He hadn't bitten his tongue hard enough.

"Alcofribas? Back already?" It was their mother. Al sprang to his feet and threw the rucksack behind the beanstalk.

"Yes, Mother. It appears that I'll need to make another attempt tomorrow."

"Oh, do try, dear. I'm sure if you return that bird that lays golden eggs, the giants will be appeased." Althea shot a disapproving glance at her younger son Jack, who was busily tying his shoe.

"Jack, you should go with him this time."

"Who, me?" he said, looking up.

"Your brother is much more responsible, that's why I've asked him to do this, but you've already been up there and can show Al where you got the duck."

"Goose," Jack corrected.

"Whatever. Just do what I tell you for a change."

"Yes, Mother."

They climbed endlessly.

The fluffy clouds didn't look like solid footing to Al, but Jack declared it was perfectly safe. They'd spent all day jumping from branch to branch and swatting at angry crows determined to drive off interlopers from their nesting heights. It was good to finally reach the top, which looked a lot like heaven.

"Let's head to that castle in the distance," Jack said. "Just follow me closely... No, not that close, man."

"Rather an odd place to live, don't you think? A castle in the clouds?" Al mused, looking around. His feet began to disappear into the white mist, then his knees.

"Looks like you're sinking," Jack observed.

"My God, help me," Al pleaded, floundering desperately like a drowning man and reaching toward Jack, who stepped back slightly.

"You've packed the rope, right?" Jack asked.

"Yes, of course! Throw it to me."

"Hmm, it's here somewhere."

"Hurry up, I'm up past my waist. If I sink through, I'll plunge to the ground."

"And that could be fatal," Jack agreed.

Now up to his chest in wet cotton wool, Al began screaming.

"Ah, here it is." Jack tossed the rope to Al, who grabbed it with a whimper.

Al was careful to step in Jack's footprints after that, before they could disappear in the fog. He didn't give a tinker's damn if he was following too close or not.

When they arrived at the castle, Jack pointed to a broken molding at the foot of the tall wooden door. "That's our in," he pronounced. "But be careful. The rats here are giants too. Not to mention the cat. I'll go first."

"Wait," Al said. "We need a plan for placating the giants about the golden goose. Perhaps grab something else we can hold for ransom?" But Jack had already jumped through the gap.

A horrible shriek pierced the air. *Jack!* Thunderous footsteps sounded near the door.

"Fum, I've got you now, Thief. We'll see how you like sitting in a bird cage. Most likely kill you in the morning."

Al hid in the darkness of the cracked molding, pulling his cape over his head and cowering until the sounds faded away. How was he going to save his brother? *Should* he save his brother, the source of all of his misery heretofore? What was he going to tell Mother if he didn't?

🌀🌀🌀

The hours crawled by, until at last the clock chimed midnight. Al counted.

"Eleven, twelve...thirteen..." No thirteen. His legs seemed to be not working at all well all of a sudden.

"Get ahold of yourself, man. You're the brains of the family. Think of something. Put one foot in front of the other. Stop talking to yourself and start moving."

Alcofribas ventured into the grand foyer and edged along the wall. Several halls led off in different directions. He'd just have to check each one until he found Jack. *If Jack was still alive.*

The first room he reached appeared to be a library. He hadn't realized that giants were literate. Or maybe they just decorated with expensively bound books, who could tell? One of those books would probably keep Al's family in food for a year, except they were too heavy to lift. He shrugged and moved on.

A soft musical sound, a beautiful, sad song floated gently from the next room, mixed with a bit of sobbing. He peeked in. A plush pink and green pastel oriental rug carpeted the floor. A lady's room, obviously. Al's stomach clenched at the thought of meeting a 16-foot woman, nice or not. Probably not nice, he thought, shrinking against the doorjamb.

The singing stopped.

"Who's that?" a voice asked. Al held his breath.

"I know you're here. I can smell you."

Well, the jig was up. All that climbing didn't exactly keep you smelling fresh as a daisy.

"I'm sorry, milady, my name is Alcofribas." After a short pause, he added, "—the Bold."

"Step into the light."

That pesky problem with his legs seemed to have returned. He managed to creep cautiously toward the pool of light cast by a crystal chandelier hanging above the center of the room. He stood there a second and turned around. No giantess. Maybe she'd given up, or he was too small to see. He started back the way he'd come.

"Another human, but not the one I expected. I thought at first you might be Jack, come to save me!" the voice said. "He promised." A quivering chord chimed in a minor key.

Al still couldn't see anyone.

"Over here, on the piano."

Al gazed upward and atop the lid of a grand piano now spotted an Irish harp, ornately sculpted with a feminine figurehead. He admired the artistically rendered bosom for a moment.

"Huh, a talking harp." He'd always wanted to play a harp. Plucked instruments were his specialty. That, and writing satirical short stories that his mother wouldn't approve of.

"I'm a *singing* harp. My name is Jamais. Come on up."

Luckily, the claw foot carved legs of the antique piano offered numerous handholds, and Al scaled one with no trouble.

"Do you know Jack?" Jamais asked. "He's extremely handsome."

"Jack's my bother, er, brother, and I'm here to save him. The giant's got him."

"Oh, could you save me too? I'm really very little trouble, and I could make you a fortune down in the human world."

"Looks like you've got a cushy gig here already," Jack said, surveying the massive, expensive furnishings.

"If by cushy you mean singing til you're hoarse every night, until your drunken tormentor passes out." She choked back a sob. "I've been stringing him along, but I don't know how much longer I can keep up this performance."

A giant's voice boomed out. "Jamais! Sing me a song while I eat a late snack."

"Hide," Jamais whispered. Al dived into the cavernous innards of the piano with a crashing tinkle.

"What was that?" the giant asked, gnawing on his sandwich. Blood dripped from the soggy deli roll, mingled with the tangy aroma of Dijon mustard. Al hadn't eaten since breakfast, and his stomach growled. The dreadful thought crossed his mind that the sandwich meat could be his brother Jack.

"Oh, I just broke a G string," Jamais replied. "I'll have it fixed in a jiffy."

"It smells wet in here," the giant said, sniffing the air. "You haven't been out traipsing in the clouds, have you?" He hoisted Jamais in the air and stared up under her base, ignoring her squeaks of modest protest. He slammed her back down on the piano.

"No, I suppose that's impossible. Oh, well, sing 'The Giant's Teeth' for me. I never can get enough of that song about the giant who was so stupid he couldn't tell there was a man living in his mouth. I'd have gulped him down before you could say toot sweet, or should I say, 'tooth sweet.' Not every giant is as smart as I am, you know."

"I'm so lucky," Jamais said. She limbered up with a two-handed glissando and launched into the tune. From his hiding place, Al was greatly impressed with its melody and lyrics. Then she played a tune about a war between the giants, in which the key to victory was getting the opponents drunk and drowning them in urine. Another song told of a giant who went to hell and left after becoming bored with it all. She played all night. Though Jamais' music was dark and hypnotic and her stories enthralling, they were also bawdy, and Al couldn't help laughing—silently—until the tears flowed. He had to admit, he was falling a little bit in love with this lovely chanteuse.

The rooster's crow breached the stone walls, signaling the eminent arrival of dawn. The giant yawned. Al hoped he'd finally go to bed.

"I'm hungry again," the giant announced. "Think I'll go see what's for breakfast."

Al climbed up to Jamais.

"What am I going to do now? Where do you suppose he has Jack?"

"If I tell you, you'll take me along, right?"

"Of course," Al promised.

"He's probably in the aviary..." she started to say, when the giant stomped back into the room.

"That human's escaped. Sound the alarm, and let me know immediately if you see him." He turned on his heel and stormed out.

Jamais trilled her best imitation of an alarm, as Al climbed back out of the piano where he had dived a second time. He slid his arm around Jamais' hardwood waist, and they clambered down the piano leg. It wasn't nearly as comfortable going down as coming up, with her zaftig charms threatening to topple them all the way. His lute callouses were beginning to wear thin.

They ran into the hallway and smack into Jack, who appeared to be making a break for the exit.

"Um, hello Jamais," Jack said, taking no notice of Al.

"Jack," she said.

"Well?" Al said.

"I've got it," Jack said, glaring at his brother. "I've got what we came for."

"But, how—? Oh, what the hell, then, let's go," Al said. They ran like the very giants of the sky were after them.

"You were just going to leave without me, weren't you?" Al accused when they were back on the ground.

"I just assumed you'd gone home," Jack said. He pulled a diamond-encrusted axe off the wall. "You should be grateful I got this baby, which is the only thing with the power to chop down the beanstalk. And now that we've got Jamais safe and sound, I think I should get to it, right, honey?"

Jamais smiled. "Right, *mon chér*."

"Alright, you fatass giants. We'll see how you like this," Jack said, dashing out the door.

"You know, I never got to thank you properly," Jamais said, pulling Al close and giving him a kiss he would never forget.

From somewhere outside in the north forty they heard Jack exclaim, "TIM-BER!" A rapid-fire barrage of chopping was followed by a deafening crash.

Alcofribas realized with a pang that he had to face facts. Jack was a big hero, and Jamais would never be his. Maybe he'd move into town, or become a hermit, or a writer. Same thing.

"Writing?" Althea wailed when told of it. In her opinion, that was only second in stupidity to selling a cow for a handful of beans.

"I'm sorry, Mother," Al said, "but I gotta be me. Besides, I picked up a lot of good material when we were up in the clouds, although some of it is rather raunchy. I may have to assume a pen name." He began sorting letters in his head for a suitable anagram.

"Hah," Jack scoffed. "You have no sense of humor, Al. You'll never make it."

"Oh, of course he will," Althea said, doing an abrupt about-face. "I'm sure you can be ribald with the best of them, dear."

Literary giant François Rabelais sat before the fire reading a story to his nephew Pierre. Jack went out to buy a bottle of cognac to celebrate his visit after so many years.

"Now, don't tire out your Uncle Al," Jamais called downstairs. Her voice was still music to François' ears. Strumming gently, Jamais fluffed up a goosefeather comforter for her famous brother-in-law.

"I won't, *Maman*," Pierre said.

"Everyone loves your stories about the giants Gargantua and Pantagruel, *mon oncle*. But—I have a question. Why didn't you ever write about how Papa rescued you and *Maman* from the beanstalk?"

*****〜〜〜*****

A New Shop!

Rosie loved to shop. She could spend hours online looking for bargains at The Find, Bluefly, or O. On Saturdays she rose early to pore through the garage sale ads in the paper. She had long ago resolved never to pay retail for anything, ever, except perhaps for her Internet service. Even so, she stopped subscribing to cable TV when she found she could use peer-to-peer networks to download music, movies, TV, and podcasts to feed her voracious entertainment appetite.

Sure, bargain hunting was a lot of work, but she wasn't afraid of that. If all you wanted to do was pay through the nose, everything you wanted could be delivered to your door. No, that was out of the question, unless it included free shipping. Rosie didn't have a job, but she knew shopping was her calling.

She bartered her garden produce at the Farmer's Market and her computer skills for visits to the personal trainer and the hair stylist. She knew how to get value without using money. Guys were always willing to share a falafel and a pint when she was spotted at microbreweries and street fairs. 117

People usually came away feeling they got a really good deal from Rosie, especially when she turned her high-wattage smile on them.

Spring was finally here. Rosie put on her strawberry bike jersey and khaki bike skort that showed off her nice white legs and prepared to pedal her cruiser to the antique shops in Niwot and Lyons. She waited until the morning rush hour traffic subsided and timed her arrival to be first as the doors would open. She hummed a Steve Miller tune as she pulled out of her driveway, "Gonna buy me a Mercury, and I'll cruise it up and down this road."

Reminded her of her racer boyfriend, Merc. Merc had overhauled her bike and put on a special headlight-looking power gizmo that made her bike faster than a nitrous-equipped Suzuki. Silly boy. He was really into speed, both motorized and pharmaceutical. At the Niwot tracks, she paused as a train approached. Although she could have jumped on the pedals to beat the train, she decided not to press her luck. The engineer let out three long blasts and waved, and she smiled as the warm air blew her hair into a fiery halo and pasted her jersey to her torso.

As she pulled into the sleepy hamlet of Niwot, she coasted past the Irish pub. A husky lad was rolling a keg of Guinness into the side door. "Hey, Rosie! We're gonna have green beer tonight," he said.

"And a happy St. Patrick's to you too," she replied, wondering what would possess someone to adulterate good beer. She never liked St. Patrick. Just a glory seeker who went around stealing the thunder of the rightful gods. She sighed. The luck of the Irish indeed.

She dismounted on Main Street and walked her bike along the shady sidewalk to survey the funky stores and coffee shops. Amazingly, there appeared to be a new shop! She tried to peer into the window, but the reflection outside made the store's interior invisible. The temptation was irresistible, and, never one to put off gratification, she parked her bike and pulled the door open. A bell jangled, followed by a long, gonglike buzz.

Fatima and Aliyah were busy stocking in the back of the shop. Aliyah glanced nervously at the sound of the door. "Our first customer. Do you think we will be able to keep her, Fatima?" Aliyah asked. Fatima replied, "Yes, of course. Just be sure to be very courteous and helpful. And patient. They aren't used to people like us." She continued tying some gold cord into a decorative noose knot for one of the ladies' outfits they sold.

Rosie didn't see anyone around in the front. It was an apparel shop of some sort. She spied a rack of shoes in the back. The music sounded like rock, but with an Eastern twang. Her eyes widened slightly as she saw a row of what looked like old-fashioned oil lamps like something out of Aladdin. So, exotic knick-knacks too. She grinned, thinking a genie's lamp would indeed be the ultimate shopper's find.

"May I help you?" a voice behind her asked. Rosie jumped and said, "Oh, hi. I just noticed your new shop. Would it be okay if I brought my bike inside? It's got a lot of bells and whistles on it, and I try to keep an eye on it."

A small dark woman with long black hair pulled back the curtain. "Yes, you are very welcome," Fatima said.

Rosie turned to try the door and discovered it locked. She swallowed the beginning pangs of an irrational claustrophobia.

"Can't get it open. Could you get the latch?"

The woman apologized, "Very sorry, the door often is sticky." Rosie popped back out and got her bike. The door closed behind again, and the loud gong resounded. It was funny the first time you heard it, but it probably got quite annoying to the shopkeeper after a while, she thought.

Rosie leaned her bike against a wall and asked, "Have you been open long?"

"About a week," the woman responded. "We came from Egypt after the uprisings and brought a number of items that we thought would make a good shop here in America."

Looking more closely, Rosie noticed the shoe rack held silk shoes with curled toes. Her shopper's radar pinged rapidly. "These slippers are nice. Do they come in sizes?"

"They should fit you well, as they have been tailored for the discriminating shopper," said the woman. A small titter seemed to come from behind the curtain. Soon another very pretty Middle Eastern girl appeared and introduced herself as Aliyah.

"Well, they certainly are pretty," Rosie said, possibly in regard to the shoes. "Do you ever take consignments or trades?"

"Oh, yes, that would be perfectly wonderful," Aliyah said. "Do you like anything you see?"

Rosie appreciatively sniffed the air. It smelled so good in here! Spices and stuff like that. Maybe Falafel?

"What? Oh, maybe I could try on one of your belly-dancing outfits there." Though Halloween was a long way off, she thought that would be a slutty yet tasteful costume. She lifted the tag on a kelly green chiffon number that would set off her hair nicely, seeing that it was $180.00. No way would she pay that. She didn't even have a Visa card, anyway. She knew it was not wise to enable herself in impulse buying, and no one had ever actually seen her debit card in person.

"All our things are of the finest quality," the woman said. "However, we knew when we saw you that you are most deserving of our richest treasures."

Rosie was flattered, but she still didn't have any *dinero*. She thought about making a graceful exit, but when she looked back toward the door, her attention went into deficit caused by a fantastic display of hats and scarves. The door wasn't where she remembered it. She must have gotten turned around looking at all the great merch.

"Would you at least like to try the outfit, madam, just to see how it would look on you? I'm sure something can be worked out if you like it."

Her boyfriend Merc would never sit still while she tried on things, but luckily he wasn't here, and the emerald sequins were a sight to behold. Rosie demurred and stepped into a tiny dressing room to wiggle into the pantaloons and bra. Well, it did fit fine, and she did have a very fine white tummy, thanks to Joe Pilates. She pulled back the curtain and gazed out into what appeared to be a large bazaar. The excellent food and spice smells were mingling with what most decidedly were smoke and manure. As she stepped outside the cubby, she was surprised when her feet met with bare dirt. She hadn't noticed that before with her shoes on.

"Oh, it looks lovely, ma'am," Fatima murmured. She held a perfectly cute pair of gold and green slippers, which Rosie wasted no time in slipping on.

Rosie noticed she was having a little trouble breathing, probably due to the tight gold piping on the costume's neckline.

"Sorry, what?" she said. She hadn't understood what Fatima was saying. And this place looked totally different than when she came in. She heard more people calling out their wares. Odd. But sometimes she was subject to migraines, which affected her vision and intensified smells. Suddenly she wasn't feeling so hot.

This shop now seemed a little too Third World for her taste. Time to exit stage left. She reached behind the cubby to retrieve her clothes, but her hand met with only a wood bench. The clothes were missing.

"We only said you look fantastic in that green outfit, Miss Rosmerta," Aliyah repeated. "Truly a goddess."

Rosie belatedly realized that these people knew her real name. That was not good. She was a little shocked, because no one had called her by that name in literally ages. She began working a protection spell. You could usually get weak-minded people to go along with you by increasing their suggestibility. "I think you will find that you have already gotten a good deal from me and return my clothes," she said. A little of the old abundance razzle-dazzle ought to do it.

"We're very sorry, Rosmerta, but we need you. We have a very nice job all worked out for you," Fatima said.

Well, that trick didn't work. She needed to get back to her bike. There it was, leaning against a flower stall. Merc had overhauled her bike and put on a special headlight-looking power gizmo that made her bike faster than a nitrous-equipped Suzuki. She grabbed the handlebars and groped for the switch on the light he had installed. Damn these migraine visuals. She didn't do well under stress. "Get me out of here," Rosie commanded, accidentally grabbing one of the oil lamps. Cursing, she threatened to throw it at the girl, though she wasn't sure where she had gotten to.

She panicked as she felt her arm rapidly turn to smoke and begin pulling her into the lamp. She clawed at the golden noose that tightened around her neck.

She screamed.

The lamp dropped to the floor and sat there unassumingly. The little shop was as it was before. A small red light on the handle blinked slowly.

Fatima beamed at Aliyah and congratulated her on the success of capturing such a beautiful Djiin. "That was very clever of you to change her headlight for a lamp," Fatima said. Aliyah batted her naturally lush lashes and smiled modestly.

"Those big Celtic goddesses are premium, aren't they," Fatima added. "Truly inspirational. And they are especially good at procuring whatever they want. She got that green outfit for practically nothing. Our customers will gladly pay for her talents as a personal shopper now that gold is in such short supply."

Aliyah agreed, and pulled a key from her bodice to lock up shop.

*****~~~~~*****

How to Become Your Witch Friend's Trusted House-Sitter

Be Thou Prepared—Witch Scouting Motto

First of all, try not to feel jealous that your friend already has moved into her own cottage in the woods, while you are still living at home in your parents' basement. Think of it as a fun opportunity to take a break from the sulfurous smells emanating from your dad's thaumic experiments. House-sitting offers a chance to experience what it's like to take care of your own place, should that ever happen…

Will you need a key? It's always good to check, because unlocking spells don't always work if the place is warded. Press the doorbell and jump back quickly. A colony of giant murder hornets behind the porch can be especially tricky. Then there's nothing for it but to run. It might be easiest to simply burrow in underground, as long as the ground is not yet frozen.

How friendly is your friend's forest abode? Agreeing to water all the plants may not be as straightforward as it seems. We recommend taking a short broom ride above the greenwood to see if there is anything dangerous creeping about down there. Of course, there WILL be, but the point is to simply be aware of things like hostile mangrove trees, quicksand, and carnivorous green slime. You might also spot some lost children wandering around in your friend's front yard. Though it's not really your responsibility, you could drop them a loaf of bread, so the little buggers can find their way out safely. But if they continue to dawdle, it's best to use your disembodied voice to shout, "Hey! Get off my friend's lawn." (Hope that advice doesn't make me sound too old.)

Is your friend's trip going to be a vacation, or is it for business? If it's business, she may not be taking her familiar along, which means you'll need to feed it every day, or more often if it's a growing dragonet. Make sure there're plenty of bunnies available in the forest for fresh meat. Unfortunately, cottage HOA rules have become increasingly strict about having livestock on the property. Just when you thought you were getting away from the pressures of the city… And while we're at it, do your familiars get along well? You've heard about dogs and cats, right? But what about dire Corgis and transmog alligators?

How long will your friend be gone? Will it be a week? A month? If your friend is being vague about it, she might be traveling in time, or she might NEVER expect to come back. Ask if your friend has a medical power of attorney or a Wytche's Wyll and who will execute it. Not to sound too mercenary, but witches have been known to get burned.

How well do you know your friend? Maybe you've been pals for years, or you may just be answering a classified ad from the university. In the latter case, this is more of a job than a favor, so for the interview, think "checklist." Take out a clipboard and tick off things like:

• Your allergies. Your so-called friend may have hexed the area to attack trespassers (remember the bees?) and inadvertently invoked something deadly. They say wolfsbane's not dangerous, but better safe than sorry.

• Your heart condition. Where's the nearest patch of foxglove? Who's the closest nearby Healer?

• Emergency contact. Get her magic mo-ball number so you can address her if needed. If you can't get a "yes-or-no" answer, you may have to resort to pyrotechnics—a flaming comet is effective but energy-intensive.

• Stock compliment. To make the best impression, do NOT tell your friend that her legs look fat in those horizontal-striped leggings.

Seal the deal by bragging a bit about how you would handle things if your feet were put to the fire.

Do pick up after yourself and leave the place in tip-top shape—even tidier than you found it. A nice, odor-concealing lavender sachet makes a perfect welcome-home present. It's not essential to let your friend know you invited your bandmates over every night, though I'm sure she'd understand that there aren't a lot of good places to practice pandemonium harp and blare-bugle without getting the neighbors in an uproar about social distancing. Clear out all booby traps. You don't want to screw up a perfectly good friendship by letting something slip through the cracks.

And finally, when your friend gets back, be prepared to listen to her travel stories and look at her pictures without gibbering hysterically. A bit of foresight goes a long way toward ensuring that your cottage-sitting experience is one that you'll both remember fondly in the future.

Maybe you'll even get to keep the key.

*****~~~~~*****

Blood Moon

Sonia Greene Drevatch splashed upstream, trying to hide her trail from her husband's bloodhounds. Stanton knew she had tried to kill him, and that she had escaped at all amazed her. She had her sturdy leather brogues to thank for that. As a Girl Guide Leader, Sonia always came prepared. She pulled the Swiss Army knife from her GG jacket and paused briefly to slash at her ballooning culottes. Modesty was the least of her worries at this point. None of her little charges were around to set a good example for, anyway.

The first drops of rain stung her face. Though it was late summer in New England, she might still die of exposure in these hurricane-season winds. Sonia choked back a sob and reminded herself that she had to be tough. She had worked out the details of the plan over many months. If she made it to the outskirts of the village of Barrington, she could find the boat hidden in the underbrush by the beach and slip into the Sound of Shelter.

"I thought I had him wrapped around my finger," Sonia thought, "but now he has to die for what he's done to me."

The first part of her plan had failed utterly. Unfortunately, Stanton Drevatch was not dead. Miraculously, he'd cast out the poison she put in his drink, enough to kill several men.

At last Sonia reached the rowboat and dug it out with wind-chilled fingers. She dragged the boat free and pushed it into the water. Climbing in, she rowed hard against the wind, wincing as blisters burned her chafed palms. She kept her back to Providence so she could watch for pursuit.

Following the black silhouette of the forested shoreline south, she disembarked at Tiverton and traced a small footpath that seemed to stretch straight upward into the trees. From the cliff top, it was a short walk to her mother's estate. Though it had been a while since they had spoken, surely her mother would give her sanctuary.

In the early dawn light, a pair of cars idled in the driveway, while men armed with machine guns milled about, as if gearing up for war. Maybe they'd heard about her escape.

"Open the gate," a deep voice boomed over the gale. It was Mathias, mother's chief bodyguard. Sonia was glad he still recognized her, soaked to the skin as she was. He lowered his tommy gun.

"Welcome home. Nice weather we're having, isn't it? Come in and get dry. What brings you back to Massachusetts again?"

"I need to talk with my mother," Sonia replied.

He nodded and gestured to his men to disperse. He eyed her bare legs but didn't mention them. Standing there, she was grateful that her old friend was familiar with her tomboy ways.

"What's going on?" Mathias asked as she sat in the kitchen sipping scalding hot coffee.

"I'd ask you the same thing," Sonia said, gesturing toward the men out front.

"I was just collecting some heat to pay a little visit to some local bootleggers who have been stirring things up. The bad weather's put the kibosh on for now, though. This 'Stinger Gang,' as they call themselves, have been a pain in the ass, stealing shipments headed for Boston and selling them. They don't realize what they're in for if the Syndicate doesn't get its cut... How are things in Providence, by the way? I should think the richest little girl in New England would have an escort." Since marrying Stanton and merging her family's distilleries with the Drevatch empire, Sonia and her widowed mother Patricia Greene had become fabulously wealthy. Though she had disapproved at first, Patricia had grown to like her daughter's charming husband and seemed pleased that business boomed in spite of Prohibition.

One of the small bells on the kitchen wall jingled. "Ah, that would be your mother," Mathias said. Sonia jumped, the cup clattering down. Pulling herself together, she boarded the small elevator to her mother's quarters and pulled the accordion gate closed.

"Sonia, my darling," her mother said, grabbing her hand and pulling her daughter into the room. "You're sopping! Come, stand closer to the gasjet. My, just look at your hands. You've really done it this time…"

"Mama, I've left Stanton," Sonia blurted. "He's an evil man. I've heard rumors that he has been expanding into racketeering in Tiverton, and I've come back to help put a stop to him."

Patricia held up her hand. "Tut, tut, not so fast. Let's not worry about that right now." She called down to Mathias for bandages for Sonia's hands. "Just get some rest, there'll be plenty of time to talk in the morning. I've left your room just as it was, so you'll be comfortable. . ." As a seeming afterthought, Patricia hugged her and added, "I love you, dear." Sonia breathed in her mother's flowery perfume and felt safe for the first time in a long while. She began to head for her bedroom.

"And Sonia…"

"Yes?"

"Get out of those dreadful rags immediately. That Girl Guide getup makes you look like a charity case."

Sonia bowed her head meekly. "Yes, Mama."

Sonia woke early the next morning and knocked on her mother's door. A maid stood brushing Patricia's silver-flecked blonde hair as she sat at the vanity. Patricia was still a handsome woman. It was no surprise that she had caught the eye of an industrial baron in her youth, Sonia thought fondly. Father hadn't even cared that she was Jewish, defying the rampant anti-Semitic attitudes in the largely white neighborhood.

"Come in, dear," Patricia said, talking to Sonia's reflection in the mirror. "What's this about a little tiff with Stanton?"

"It's not a tiff. I tried to kill him."

"What?!"

"I poisoned him, but he must have had an antidote, or maybe he used leeches to suck out the toxin. At any rate, I botched it."

Wide-eyed, Patricia waved the maid away and turned to face Sonia.

"You've got to go back. Go to your room and start getting your things together. You'll return when the weather improves. You've got to put aside those childish delusions of yours. You must keep your promise as a wife—and don't forget you're a Board member. We have to keep up appearances. We'll think of some sort of excuse for the poison—that it was an accident with the wrong tea, or something. I'll have Mathias accompany you."

"But—" Sonia tried to object.

"Go on, we'll work it out somehow."

Sonia walked back to her room, shaken. It was her own fault. Headstrong, she had thrown herself at Stanton, although her mother discouraged the union. *Strange to find her now obviously in thrall to the man.* Sonia wasn't sure what to do. She sat on the bed and briefly considered what she would pack. Seeing the normal street clothes in her closet made her recall the days before her marriage last year. Stanton had insisted she wear the olive drab Girl Guide Leader uniform to Board meetings to give the false impression that the Drevatch Syndicate was a respectable business with ties to the community. She hadn't minded play acting at first, and was even proud of the dozen badges sewn onto her sleeves. The wilderness survival badge in particular had come in handy. She was a real Girl Guide now.

No. I am not going to pack, and I am not going to go back. I didn't agree to be Stanton's pawn, or to be window dressing for his illegal enterprise. I'll have my independence.

Sonia walked out to the garden to clear her head. She'd always loved the sun-drenched haven, with its colorful flowers and neatly trimmed topiaries. Now she found it overgrown with weeds and strewn with bits of junk.

How long had she been gone?

Velvety parasitic red insects busily lay their eggs on the larvae of other ground-nesting wasps. Sonia knew their paralytic sting was painful enough to kill a full-grown cow. Instead of feeding the cycle of life, Death itself, or something totally antithetical to life, was killing everything, spreading destruction and famine to what once was her future. She stepped on one of the velvet wasps, which buried its stinger into her Cuban heel shoe before it succumbed with a death rattle. Disoriented and confused, she went back upstairs to don her scouting jacket and sensible footwear. She reached under the bed for one last thing, a medical kit. She had used the hypodermic needle to administer her father's morphine shots when he was dying. Her poor mother had been too squeamish to do it.

She was on her own now. She consulted her pocket watch and rehearsed what she would say to Patricia, that she'd catch a ride back with Mathias. Her arrival yesterday had postponed his foray, and she now found the grizzled veteran regathering henchmen and weapons and loading them into her mother's big black Packard.

"Mathias, may I talk to you?"

"Sure, Sonia."

"Can you tell me more about this gang that you're after?"

"Only that they are a bunch of ex-farmers who decided to help themselves to what ain't theirs. Patricia wants us to persuade them to desist."

"How many of them are there?"

"No one really knows. There can't be very many, though, and I think it won't be too much trouble to clean them out, once we find their hideout."

"I'd like to accompany you on the scouting party," Sonia said. Maybe these ruffians could recruited to fight Stanton, she thought.

"Fat chance. Your mother wouldn't allow it. If one little hair of your pretty little head was harmed—"

Perhaps, but obviously her mother wasn't going to go against Stanton. Besides, she didn't live here any more. "Mother doesn't need to know about this. It's important I find out about this gang—what do they call themselves— the Stinger Gang?"

"It could be quite dangerous, Sonia."

"I have a Self Defense badge, Mathias," she said, pointing to her sleeve. "And I'm sure that my tracking skills would be useful for finding these people. Please, you've helped me lots of times before…"

Mathias chuckled, rubbing the brim of his fedora while he thought, a good sign. He finally assented and held the door open for her.

"But you stay in the car," he ordered. Sonia nodded, fingers crossed behind her back.

Sonia, Mathias, and four men drove out of the compound heading east into the Berkshires, where the hilly forest offered many hiding places for criminals. At the top of the fifth step climb, they got out to stretch their legs and let the radiators cool. They'd spent most of the day, coming up empty. Mathias lit a cigarette and blew a lazy smoke ring. A high-pitched snick of breaking glass drew his attention to the spidered hole that had just appeared in the windshield.

Mathias's warning yell shattered the quiet. He pulled out his pistol and gestured to Sonia to hide. From the cover of the trees, she heard the sound of gunshots echoing behind her.

It was a long way, but she began to hike cross country to get help. Struggling through woods smelling of mud and wet leaves, Sonia hoped Mathias and his cohort would still be alive when she returned with backup.

Sonia felt a blow at her back, knocking the wind out of her. She tried to turn and scream, but a big hand covered her nose and mouth. She bit into the hand and heard ferocious cursing, but there wasn't enough time to devise a defense. She stubbornly fought to stay conscious, but a suffocating shadow took her.

Opening her eyes, Sonia found she couldn't move her hands, which were tied behind her back. She lay on her side, unsure how much time had passed. She wasn't dead, at any rate. A campfire reflected yellow off the ochre walls of a cave.

"Goddamn you," Sonia swore, her voice hoarse. "My mother will have your heads, you bastards. Let me loose at once!"

"Tut, tut," a voice said. "Not very ladylike language. I see you've woke up."

"Who are you?" Sonia demanded.

"Howard Ballard, at your service."

He didn't look—or smell—like a farmer, but who else could it be?

"Are you one of the Stinger bootleggers?"

"Oh, you've heard of us? But as to bootlegger, I like to think of myself as a patriot. Yes, I'm in the S.G. Perhaps you could share with us who you are? I've not heard of any Girl Guide campouts in these woods lately."

"I'm not here to camp. I'm here to help. Patricia Portwine Greene is my mother. I want to clean out Stanton Drevatch's illegal business. For some reason Mother tolerates his Syndicate, and has let him take over the family business." Sonia thought it best for the moment not to mention that Stanton was her husband.

"She doesn't just tolerate it—she supports it," Howard asserted.

"What happened to my escort?" Sonia demanded. She couldn't believe she had actually looked for these people. Maybe Ballard's gang weren't bootleggers, but they were definitely gun-toting kidnappers.

"You mean Mathias? He hightailed it out, probably to go tattle to your mother. Don't worry, we won't hold you for ransom."

Surely a lie, she suspected. *But he seems to know everything about us. Maybe she could stall until she had a strategy for escape.*

"Why do you call yourselves the Stinger Gang?" Something about the name gnawed at the back of her mind.

"Me and my buddies raid Drevatch's shipments, stinging them where it hurts most. You can call us vigilantes, but I don't care."

"Drevatch recruits workers, offering high wages, but no one ever manages to collect," Howard said harshly.

He described rumors that Stanton was luring them somehow and then killing them. "I think he is stockpiling blood for some nefarious purpose.

Sonia had never seen Stanton engage in anything so vile as vampirism. Her mind raced, trying to recall what had happened in the past year. It was all a blur. She wondered aloud if she had been a victim herself.

"But he isn't a vampire," Howard said. "He's something worse."

Sonia felt a pang of dread, and her pulse quickened. With new resolve, she asked, "May I stay?"

Over the next few months, the Stinger Gang stepped up its patrols of the county, encountering new scenes of devastation. One village had been burned completely. The acrid smell of gasoline and decaying corpses assaulted their senses, the unwholesome evidence only half-concealed. Most of the inhabitants had fled or vanished. The few wandering survivors seemed to have no memory and could tell them little.

"More of the same, eh?" Sonia said, poking through the charred rubble of a farmstead. Since joining the gang, she was finally feeling like one of the S.G.—at least comfortable enough to share her thoughts with Howard.

"Obviously Stanton's doing," Howard asserted. "When we first met, you told me how he mistreated you. He's got some sort of memory control. Plus, I'm sure he killed my brother."

"Your brother? When did that happen?" Sonia asked, aghast that Howard had kept this to himself all this time.

"Like I've told you before, my brother disappeared nearly a year ago. He and his bride were on their way to their honeymoon when they probably stumbled on one of Drevatch's dirty dealings. We looked for a week but only found his blood-soaked velvet vest."

A year. That was about how long Sonia had been married. She didn't recall ever telling Howard about Stanton's mistreatment. The holes in her memory frustrated her, because like the villagers she could recall only bits and pieces of the year beyond—she realized with a gasp—her wedding night. That night in the bedroom, Stanton had discarded his disguise. His normally blue eyes glowed a sickly green. He pinned her arms and stared intently into her eyes, his mesmerizing gaze causing her to sleep and forget all memories for days. Until recently, the few memories she had were of Stanton giving her a kiss and pushing her into the Boardroom to serve coffee. Adding to the insult, she kept forgetting that she had repeatedly run away, and more importantly, why she had tried to kill the lying crook. He had stolen a year of her life.

At the next raid, the Stinger Gang were careful to stay upwind of Stanton's red fumes, and gradually they regained lost ground.

When spring returned, Howard and Sonia walked to a secluded spot outside the camp to discuss further strategies. The waterfall near the cave was thawing, cascading into a small lake. "They say this is the clearest water in the world," Howard said.

"I didn't know you were such an expert," she said, her eyes twinkling. She scooped some of the icy water with her hand and offered it to him. He drank eagerly, then pulled her closer.

"Hey, I'm a married woman," she half-protested. Suddenly her Girl Guide jacket felt much too warm. She lifted her badge-filled sash over her head, and Howard threw it aside. They fell to the ground, rolling and entwining. Later, as they lay resting in each other's arms after their exertions, Howard stroked Sonia's hair and spoke.

"Now that summer's coming, it's time to take back your mother's compound and repel the Drevatch Syndicate for good," he said.

Sonia shuddered at the thought of ever laying eyes on Stanton again, but she agreed, murmuring, "I suppose we will have to." They gathered their scattered clothes and headed back to the camp.

A low moan alerted Sonia and Howard. An open pit yawned in the forest floor, its camouflage of leaves and branches tossed asunder. The S.G.'s concealed trap had finally caught one of Stanton's lieutenants. He screamed as they hauled him out, his leg dangling at a sickening angle. It took little convincing before he revealed that Stanton's men burned a special incense in a thurible and swung it around to befuddle the Berkshire villagers, who were then easily captured.

"What does Drevatch do with the captives?" Howard demanded.

"I don't know," the marauder said. "I swear."

"Let him go," Howard said. To the captive, he said, "Tell the monster his days are numbered." The man shambled away. No one offered to help him.

Sonia asked, "Are you sure it was a good idea to let him go?"

"He probably knows less than we do," Howard responded. "Besides, Stanton will certainly kill him for getting caught anyway. At least his death won't be on my conscience."

This was their chance to get the upper hand, but when they returned to camp, an ambush was under way. Sonia was soon too busy to say, "I told you so." Stanton's men had tossed grenades of red smoke into the camp, and many of the S.G. lay on the ground, coughing and retching.

She turned to see Howard fall. Stanton strode into the camp and towered over him. Stanton cast a fervid smile in her direction before ordering his men to take Howard prisoner.

Desperate, she fled to the road and hitchhiked back to her mother's. She felt like an idiot, but blood was thicker than… She rang at the gate.

Patricia herself appeared. "Stanton called and said you'd be coming."

She was much changed since Sonia had seen her only a few months earlier. Dark circles ringed her eyes, creases traced her face, and her fashionable silk dress was dirty and hung loosely.

Sonia once again found herself in the humiliating position of begging for her mother's help. She stood in Patricia's foyer, guarded by Mathias. A display of lethal weapons hung on the walls. Sonia wrenched her eyes away.

"Mother, Stanton has ambushed the Stinger Gang and taken their leader prisoner."

"You think I don't know that?" Patricia replied. "And obviously you're the deranged Girl Guide traipsing about the woods?"

"I've heard you knew all along about Stanton," Sonia said. "Why didn't you tell me?"

"I didn't think you needed that information."

"What? I was nothing but an empty vessel slowly filling with Stanton's corruption. What happened to me? I want answers, Mother."

"I did my best to protect you and your little gang from Stanton's harm," Patricia said. "But to tell the truth, I've grown to wish I'd never had a daughter. Your father always spoiled you, and then Stanton wanted you for your beauty and connections, and I was forced to let him have you. The worst part was that you kept running away, and I had to send you back." Her normally imperious voice trembled.

Bewildered by her mother's anger and jealousy, Sonia hesitated.

"I know you're allied with Stanton, but you've got to help us. Or if not us, you've got to help all the innocent people he's killing," Sonia pleaded. "Please. You were born here. Help your own people." There was no reply. She felt her face turn red. "All right, I'll have to defeat him myself, then," she said, and turned to go.

"Stop, you stupid girl," her mother said. "Stanton is a blood sorcerer. He once was buried alive by his fellows, but he managed to escape. He vowed to seek revenge. Our family blood contains the key ingredient in his bait and makes him virtually unkillable. He had a ready supply when he married you, and you never knew it. When you ran off, he started taking mine. You've been the death of me. Soon you'll also be the death of this whole county."

Patricia raised a revolver. Sonia held up her hands.

"Please, Mother, don't..." But instead of shooting at Sonia, Patricia put the gun to her head and fired. She dropped to the floor, knocking over a nearby table and scattering papers and photographs.

"No!" Sonia cried. Penitent, she crawled over to her mother's side. Sobbing, Sonia brushed back the locks of blood-drenched blonde hair that tumbled across Patricia's face. She was so thin, almost a skeleton. Patricia had abetted Stanton, that was true, but she had also secretly extended her protection to the S.G. Her mother's protection had died with her, and Sonia was on her own again.

"I'm so sorry, Mother."

Patricia had called her "the death of this whole county." Sonia turned to Mathias. He cringed, as if expecting a bolt of punishment. "What did she mean about me, Mathias?" Mathias turned on his heel and ran from the room.

Mathias had been like a father to her. Shocked by his cowardly behavior, Sonia groaned as memories poured back. Disconsolate, she surveyed the papers lying about her mother and reached for the nearest one, a black-and-white photograph. It captured in perfect focus an appalling pile of dead bodies. Riveted, she rifled through the other photos. Girl Guide campers, lying in pools of black blood. Sonia was all too familiar with the uniform. Had Stanton and her mother murdered these young girls? It was already too much, but there was plenty more where that came from. The penultimate picture showed a gruesome closeup of a murdered man, his hand holding a crushed white carnation, as a pair of feminine ankles stood off to the side. *Her* ankles, wearing Sonia's favorite white socks with the frilly cuffs. Unwilling to uncover her eyes, she stared at the last one. *I'm in the photograph with Howard's brother.* Now, she knew why her mother had killed herself. Patricia had been driven insane by the proof of her daughter's foul deeds. Sonia struggled to her feet and began limping in the direction Mathias had taken.

She looked up and saw Howard running toward her. Thank God, he had escaped. But that might mean that Stanton was already here too. *Yes.* She heard Stanton's hateful hounds baying in front of the gate.

"Sonia, I came to warn you," Howard panted. "That bastard bragged about the death of my brother and said he is powerful enough now from the blood of his slaves. He babbled about being a Servant of the Old Ones and getting back in their good graces. He is coming to take you back… My God, is that your mother?"

Sonia pulled him away, unwilling—and unable—to explain, and they ran outside into the courtyard, where Mathias fought off a pack of unruly dogs. He wasn't such a coward, after all.

"Sleep," Sonia ordered. Stanton's hounds desisted and lay quiet. She felt a seed of satisfaction that she had picked up the mesmerizing technique her husband had constantly used on her.

"We'll get Stanton together," Howard said. He signaled to Matthias.

"Wait. Let me talk to him first," Sonia said. Howard had no idea that she was part of the evil that he faced, and she wanted to keep it that way.

He nodded. "If he tries anything, I'll…" But she was already gone.

Dusk signaled the approach of night, but a full moon rose, making a stealthy approach difficult. Sonia slipped outside the compound and circled around to Stanton's rear, upwind of his smoking thuribles. He was engrossed in exhorting men armed with sledgehammers to demolish the rear gate. A red fog crept across the moon in a rare lunar eclipse, bathing the courtyard in a gory light. The men stopped working and stared upward at the blood moon. Now Sonia remembered what she came to do. For once, she had the element of surprise.

She patted the leather pouch at her waist. It was still there. Taking care to avoid Stanton's gaze, she charged. She plunged her father's hypodermic into her husband's chest. The first thrust rebounded off one of his ribs, nearly knocking the needle from her hand. Weeping, she tried again, jabbing him in the throat and pressing the plunger. This time the stinger found its mark.

"I found a new formula, Stanton. I hope you like it. It's venom from the Red Velvet wasp." Red light reflected from the choroid of his moonstruck eyes, as he fought against the poison burning him from within. He dropped the thurible and slumped forward, truly dead this time.

Freed of Stanton's dominion, Sonia could go anywhere she wanted now. She *should* go back to Howard. He worshipped the ground she walked on. She was sure he would agree that the past was better forgotten. But there were still too many questions. Questions she couldn't answer. Was she, like Stanton, a servant of evil? Was the blood moon a sign of the End Times? She looked at her hands and could discern no blood on them, only invisible guilt. Until she remembered it *all,* she wasn't really free.

By now, Howard had undoubtedly discovered the photographs. Broken, Sonia slid to the ground, her mind consumed by the single horror: "Whose creature am I now?"

*****~~~~~*****

Credits and Acknowledgments

Editor and Publisher – Juliana Rew, Sophont Press

Cover image and design – Keely Rew

Ebook only:

"The Twelfth Witch" – The flight of Madeline and Porphyro during the drunkenness attending the revelry (The Eve of St. Agnes), William Holman Hunt, Google Art Project.jpg|

"Rage, Rage…" Night sky with stars, beside a tree silhouette – commons.wikimedia.org Work by Michael J. Bennett

"A New Shop" – Cycles Gladiator ad by Georges Massias, circa 1895. Public domain in US. Commons.wikimedia.org

Clip art:

"The Twelfth Witch" – Magical Lady and Bird - Based on Howard Pyle 1904 drawing. Public domain, from OpenClipArt.org

"Banish Mishanter" – Alloway Kirk, Scotland. Engraving by Capt. Francis Grose, made at the request of the poet Robert Burns, in return for which Burns wrote the poem Tam o' Shanter to accompany the illustration. Grose wrote, "This church is also famous for being the place wherein the witches and warlocks used to hold infernal meetings, or sabbaths, and prepare their magical unctions; here too they used to amuse themselves with dancing to the pipes of the muckle-horned Deel. Diverse stories of these horrid rites are still current: one of which my worthy friend Mr. Burns has here favoured me with in verse." Source: *The Antiquities Of Scotland*. Commons. Wikimedia.org, public domain

All other images – royalty-free stock art

Stories about "The Twelfth Witch" first appeared in the *Arcane Arts Anthology*. "The Wet at the Top of the Stairs" first appeared in *Infective Ink*. "The Horrible and Terrifying Deeds of Alcofribas the Bold, Son of the Widow Althea, of Whom Little Is Known," won Honorable Mention at the Writers of the Future Contest and won the slush read at MileHiCon. "A New Shop!" first appeared in *Hogglepot Journal*.

*****〜〜〜〜〜*****

About Juliana Rew

Juliana Rew is a former science and technical writer for the National Center for Atmospheric Research and the Geological Society of America. She has won over a dozen technical writing competitions, and is a software engineer by training. She also publishes fantasy and science fiction by other authors at Third Flatiron Publishing. For more information about her books, visit her author website, www.julianarew.com.

*****〜〜〜〜〜*****

Twelve All in Dread

Discover other titles by Juliana Rew:

The Unwinding: Gin's Story - Book 1, The Unwinding

Korean-American housewife Virginia Sun-Jones and her husband are enjoying a Christmas picnic on the North Carolina beach with their newly married daughter and son-in-law, when a shattering cosmic event, the "Unwinding," rips them all apart. Caught in a duel between warring universes, Gin embarks on a cosmic quest to be reunited with her   family.

"A sci-fi romp that's vast in scale yet thoroughly playful.**"—Kirkus Reviews**
Extremophile: Violet Rain - Book 2, The Unwinding

Violet Rain, a VR expert from the 25th century, joins the crew of time-traveling Watchmen, monitoring the precarious truce between universes ("The Unwinding: Gin's Story") from a remote space station. Engineering a rugged tardigrade body to temporarily host her through the extreme conditions of space, she detects a new abnormality and fears a new Unwinding.

Lucanus: Prodigal Son – Book 3, The Unwinding

The cosmic disruption known as The Unwinding leaves the galaxy's scattered survivors to pick up the pieces. The tine-traveling Watchmen discover an unlikely ally in Lucanus, the renegade son of the   Masquat   Empire.

The Adventures of Mountain Ma'am

Historical fantasy set in post-Civil War Colorado Territory. Struggling to survive in the treacherous mountains above Leadville, Colorado, Callie Dawson never expected to find a friend--let alone a partner. But when she befriends a wild dwolf, Sina, Callie learns she has a destiny intertwined with the future of the American West. She is the   Mountain   Ma'am!
Silver   Medal   award,   Coffee   Pot   Book   Club